A PUFFIN BOOK

PROPERTY OF

_____

_____

E. B. WHITE was born in Mount Vernon, New York. He graduated from Cornell University in 1921, then travelled about trying many sorts of jobs, and finally joined the *New Yorker* magazine. He kept animals on his farm in Maine, and some of these creatures crept into his stories and books. In 1970, Mr White received the Laura Ingalls Wilder Award, given every five years for substantial and lasting contributions to children's literature by the American Library Association.

E. B. White died in 1985.

Books by E. B. White

CHARLOTTE'S WEB
STUART LITTLE
THE TRUMPET OF THE SWAN

E. B. WHITE

Stuart Little

Illustrated by Garth Williams

A PUFFIN BOOK

Peng   USA
Penguin Gro   da M4P 2Y3

Penguin   oks Ltd)
Peng   ralia

Penguin Boo   o 017, India
Pen   nd
(a division of Pearson New Zealand Ltd)
Penguin Books (South Africa) (Pty) Ltd, Block D, Rosebank Office Park,
181 Jan Smuts Avenue, Parktown North, Gauteng 2193, South Africa

Penguin Books Ltd, Registered Offices: 80 Strand, London WC2R ORL, England

puffinbooks. com

First published in the USA 1945
Published in Great Britain by Hamish Hamilton 1946
Published in Puffin Books 1969
Reissued in this edition 2014
004

Copyright 1945 by E. B. White
Text copyright renewed © E. B. White, 1973
Illustrations copyright renewed © Garth Williams, 1973
All rights reserved

Set in 13.5/20.5pt Sabon LT Std
Made and printed in England by Clays Ltd, St Ives plc

British Library Cataloguing in Publication Data
A CIP catalogue record for this book is available from the British Library

ISBN: 978-0-141-35483-5

www.greenpenguin.co.uk

MIX
Paper from
responsible sources
FSC
www.fsc.org   **FSC™ C018179**

Penguin Books is committed to a sustainable
future for our business, our readers and our planet.
This book is made from Forest Stewardship
Council™ certified paper.

Contents

Contents

1. In the Drain

WHEN Mrs Frederick C. Little's second son arrived, everybody noticed that he was not much bigger than a mouse. The truth of the matter was, the baby looked very much like a mouse in every way. He was only about two inches high; and he had a mouse's sharp nose, a mouse's tail, a mouse's whiskers, and the pleasant, shy manner of a mouse. Before he was many days old he was not only looking like a mouse but acting like one, too – wearing a grey hat and carrying a small cane. Mr and Mrs Little named him Stuart, and Mr Little made him a tiny bed out of four clothespins and a cigarette box.

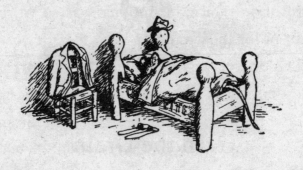

Unlike most babies, Stuart could walk as soon as he was born. When he was a week old he could climb lamps by shinnying up the cord. Mrs Little saw right away that the infant clothes she had provided were unsuitable, and she set to work and made him a fine little blue worsted suit with patch pockets in which he could keep his handkerchief, his money, and his keys. Every morning, before Stuart dressed, Mrs Little went into his room and weighed him on a small scale which was really meant for weighing letters. At birth Stuart could have been sent by first class mail for three cents, but his parents preferred to keep him rather than send him away; and when, at the age of a month, he had gained only a third of an ounce, his mother was so worried she sent for the doctor.

The doctor was delighted with Stuart and said that it was very unusual for an American family to have a mouse. He took Stuart's temperature and found that it was 98.6, which is normal for a mouse. He also examined Stuart's chest and heart and looked into his ears solemnly with a flashlight. (Not every doctor can look into a mouse's ear without laughing.) Everything seemed to be all right, and Mrs Little was pleased to get such a good report.

'Feed him up!' said the doctor cheerfully, as he left.

The home of the Little family was

a pleasant place near a park in New York City. In the mornings the sun streamed in through the east windows, and all the Littles were up early as a general rule. Stuart was a great help to his parents, and to his older brother George, because of his small size and because he could do things that a mouse can do and was agreeable about doing them. One day when Mrs Little was washing out the bathtub after Mr Little had taken a bath, she lost a ring off her finger and was horrified to discover that it had fallen down the drain.

'What had I better do?' she cried, trying to keep the tears back.

'If I were you,' said George, 'I should bend a hairpin in the shape of a fishhook and tie it on to a piece of string and try to fish the ring out with it.' So Mrs Little found a piece of string and a hairpin, and for about a half-hour she fished for the ring; but it was dark down the drain and the hook always seemed to catch on something before she could get it down to where the ring was.

'What luck?' inquired Mr Little, coming into the bathroom.

'No luck at all,' said Mrs Little. 'The ring is so far down I can't fish it up.'

'Why don't we send Stuart down after it?' suggested Mr Little. 'How about it, Stuart, would you like to try?'

'Yes, I would,' Stuart replied, 'but I think I'd better get into my old pants. I imagine it's wet down there.'

'It's all of that,' said George, who was a trifle annoyed that his hook idea hadn't worked. So Stuart slipped into his old pants and prepared to go down the drain after the ring. He decided to carry the string along with him, leaving one end in charge of his father. 'When I jerk three times on the string, pull me up,' he said. And while Mr Little knelt in the tub, Stuart slid easily down the drain and was

lost to view. In
a minute or so,
there came three
quick jerks on the
string, and Mr Little carefully hauled it up.
There, at the end, was Stuart, with the ring
safely around his neck.

'Oh, my brave little son,' said Mrs Little
proudly, as she kissed Stuart and thanked
him.

'How was it down there?' asked Mr Little,
who was always curious to know about places
he had never been to.

'It was all right,' said Stuart.

But the truth was the drain had made him very slimy, and it was necessary for him to take a bath and sprinkle himself with a bit of his mother's violet water before he felt himself again. Everybody in the family thought he had been awfully good about the whole thing.

2. Home Problems

STUART was also helpful when it came to Ping-pong. The Littles liked Ping-pong, but the balls had a way of rolling under chairs, sofas, and radiators, and this meant that the players were forever stooping down and reaching under things. Stuart soon learned to chase balls, and it was a great sight to see him come out from under a hot radiator, pushing a Ping-pong ball with all his might, the perspiration rolling down his cheeks. The ball, of course, was almost as high as he was, and he had to throw his whole weight against it

in order to keep it
rolling.

The Littles had a
grand piano in their
living room, which
was all right except

that one of the keys was a sticky key and
didn't work properly. Mrs Little said she
thought it must be the damp weather, but I
don't see how it could be the damp weather,
for the key had been sticking for about four
years, during which time there had been many
bright clear days. But anyway, the key stuck,
and was a great inconvenience to anyone
trying to play the piano. It bothered George
particularly when he was playing the 'Scarf
Dance,' which was rather lively. It was George
who had the idea of stationing Stuart inside
the piano to push the key up the second it was
played. This was no easy job for Stuart, as he
had to crouch down between the felt hammers
so that he wouldn't get hit on the head. But

Stuart liked it just the same: it was exciting inside the piano, dodging about, and the noise was quite terrific. Sometimes after a long session he would emerge quite deaf, as though he had just stepped out of an airplane after a long journey; and it would be some little time before he really felt normal again.

Mr and Mrs Little often discussed Stuart quietly between themselves when he wasn't around, for they had never quite recovered from the shock and surprise of having a mouse in the family. He was so very tiny and he presented so many problems to his parents. Mr Little said that, for one thing, there must be no references to 'mice' in their conversation. He made Mrs Little tear from the nursery songbook the page about the 'Three Blind Mice, See How They Run.'

'I don't want Stuart to get a lot of notions in his head,' said Mr Little. 'I should feel badly to have my son grow up fearing that a farmer's wife was going to cut off his tail with a carving knife. It is such things that make children dream bad dreams when they go to bed at night.'

'Yes,' replied Mrs Little, 'and I think we had better start thinking about the poem " 'Twas the night before Christmas when all through the house not a creature was stirring, not even a mouse." I think it might embarrass Stuart to hear mice mentioned in such a belittling manner.'

'That's right,' said her husband, 'but what shall we say when we come to that line in the poem? We'll have to say *some*thing. We can't just say " 'Twas the night before Christmas when all through the house not a creature was stirring." That doesn't sound complete; it needs a word to rhyme with house.'

'What about louse?' asked Mrs Little.

'Or grouse,' said Mr Little.

'I suggest souse,' remarked George, who had been listening to the conversation from across the room.

It was decided that louse was the best substitute for mouse, and so when Christmas came around Mrs Little carefully rubbed out the word mouse from the poem and wrote in the word louse, and Stuart always thought that the poem went this way:

> *'Twas the night before Christmas when all*
> *through the house*
> *Not a creature was stirring, not even a louse.*

The thing that worried Mr Little most was the mousehole in the pantry. This hole had been made by some mice in the days before the Littles came to live in the house, and nothing had been done about stopping it up. Mr Little was not at all sure that he understood Stuart's real feeling about a mousehole. He didn't know where the hole led to, and it made him uneasy to think that Stuart might some day feel the desire to venture into it.

'After all, he does look a good deal like a mouse,' said Mr Little to his wife. 'And I've never seen a mouse yet that didn't like to go into a hole.'

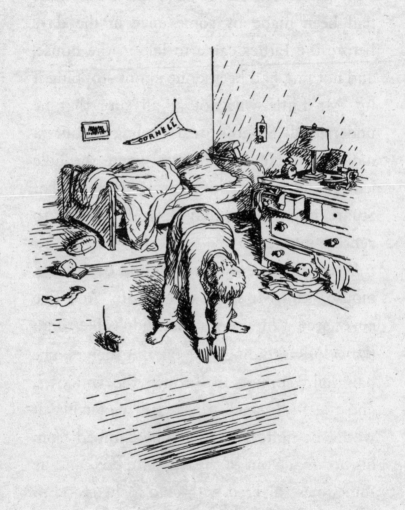

3. Washing Up

STUART was an early riser: he was almost always the first person up in the morning. He liked the feeling of being the first one stirring; he enjoyed the quiet rooms with the books standing still on the shelves, the pale light coming in through the windows, and the fresh smell of day. In wintertime it would be quite dark when he climbed from his bed made out of the cigarette box, and he sometimes shivered with cold as he stood in his nightgown doing his exercises. (Stuart touched his toes ten times every morning to keep himself in good condition. He had seen his brother George do it, and George had explained that it kept the stomach muscles firm and was a fine abdominal thing to do.)

After exercising, Stuart would slip on his handsome wool wrapper, tie the cord tightly around his waist, and start for the bathroom, creeping silently through the long dark hall past his mother's and father's room, past the hall closet where the carpet sweeper was kept, past George's room, and along by the head of the stairs till he got to the bathroom.

Of course, the bathroom would be dark, too, but Stuart's father had thoughtfully tied a long string to the pull-chain of the light. The string reached clear to the floor. By grasping it as high up as he could and throwing his whole weight on it, Stuart was able to turn on the light. Swinging on the string this way, with his long bathrobe trailing around his ankles, he looked like a little old friar pulling the bellrope in an abbey.

To get to the washbasin, Stuart had to climb a tiny rope ladder which his father had fixed for him. George had promised to build Stuart a small special washbasin only one inch high and with a little rubber tube through which water would flow; but George was always saying that he was going to build something and then forgetting about it. Stuart just went ahead and climbed the rope ladder to the family washbasin every morning to wash his face and hands and brush his teeth. Mrs Little had provided him with a doll's size toothbrush, a doll's size cake of soap, a doll's size washcloth, and a doll's comb – which he used for combing his whiskers. He carried these things in his bathrobe pocket, and when he reached the top of the ladder he took them out, laid them neatly in a row, and set about the task of turning the water on. For such a small fellow, turning the water on was quite a problem. He had discussed it with his father one day after making several unsuccessful attempts.

'I can get up onto the faucet all right,' he explained, 'but I can't seem to turn it on, because I have nothing to brace my feet against.'

'Yes, I know,' his father replied, 'that's the whole trouble.'

George, who always listened to conversations whenever he could, said that in his opinion they ought to construct a brace for Stuart; and with that he got out some boards, a saw, a hammer, a screwdriver, a bradawl, and some nails, and started to make a terrific fuss in the bathroom, building what he said was going to be a brace for Stuart. But he soon became interested in something else and disappeared, leaving the tools lying around all over the bathroom floor.

Stuart, after examining this mess, turned to his father again. 'Maybe I could pound the faucet with something and turn it on that way,' he said.

So Stuart's father provided him with a very small, light hammer made of wood; and Stuart found that by swinging it three times around his head and letting it come down with a crash against the handle of the faucet, he could start a thin stream of water flowing – enough to brush his teeth in, anyway, and moisten his washcloth. So every morning, after climbing

to the basin, he would seize his hammer and pound the faucet, and the other members of the household, dozing in their beds, would hear the bright sharp *plink plink plink* of Stuart's hammer, like a faraway blacksmith, telling them that day had come and that Stuart was trying to brush his teeth.

4. Exercise

ONE fine morning in the month of May when Stuart was three years old, he arose early as was his custom, washed and dressed himself, took his hat and cane, and went downstairs into the living room to see what was doing. Nobody was around but Snowbell, the white cat belonging to Mrs Little. Snowbell was another early riser, and this morning he was lying on the rug in the middle of the room, thinking about the days when he was just a kitten.

'Good morning,' said Stuart.

'Hello,' replied Snowbell, sharply. 'You're up early, aren't you?'

Stuart looked at his watch. 'Yes,' he said, 'it's only five minutes past six, but I felt good and I thought I'd come down and get a little exercise.'

'I should think you'd get all the exercise you want up there in the bathroom, banging around, waking all the rest of us up trying to get that water started so you can brush your teeth. Your teeth aren't really big enough to brush anyway. Want to see a good set? Look at mine!' Snowbell opened his mouth and showed two rows of gleaming white teeth, sharp as needles.

'Very nice,' said Stuart. 'But mine are all right, too, even though they're small. As for exercise, I take all I can get. I bet my stomach muscles are firmer than yours.'

'I bet they're not,' said the cat.

'I bet they are,' said Stuart. 'They're like iron bands.'

'I bet they're not,' said the cat.

Stuart glanced around the room to see what he could do to prove to Snowbell what good stomach muscles he had. He spied the drawn window shade on the east window, with its shade cord and ring, like a trapeze, and it gave him an idea. Climbing to the windowsill he took off his hat and laid down his cane.

'You can't do this,' he said to the cat. And he ran and jumped on to the ring, the way acrobats do in a circus, meaning to pull himself up.

A surprising thing happened. Stuart had taken such a hard jump that it started the shade: with a loud snap the shade flew up clear to the top of the window, dragging Stuart along with it and rolling him up inside, so that he couldn't budge.

'Holy mackerel!' said Snowbell, who was almost as surprised as Stuart Little. 'I guess that will teach him to show off his muscles.'

'Help! Let me out!' cried Stuart, who was frightened and bruised inside the rolled-up shade, and who could hardly breathe. But his voice was so weak that nobody heard. Snowbell just chuckled. He was not fond of Stuart and it didn't bother him at all that Stuart was all wrapped up in a window shade, crying and hurt and unable to get out. Instead of running upstairs and telling Mr and Mrs Little about the accident, Snowbell did a very curious thing. He glanced around to see if anybody was looking, then he leapt softly to the windowsill, picked up Stuart's hat and

cane in his mouth, carried them to the pantry
and laid them down at the entrance to the
mousehole.

When Mrs Little came down later and
found them there, she gave a shrill scream
which brought everybody on the run.

'It's happened,' she cried.

'What has?' asked her husband.

'Stuart's down the mousehole.'

5. Rescued

GEORGE was in favour of ripping up the pantry floor. He ran and got his hammer, his screwdriver, and an ice pick.

'I'll have this old floor up in double-quick time,' he said, inserting his screwdriver under the edge of the first board and giving a good vigorous pry.

'We will *not* rip up this floor till we have had a good search,' announced Mr Little. 'That's final, George! You can put that hammer away where you got it.'

'Oh, all right,' said George. 'I see that nobody in this house cares anything about Stuart but me.'

Mrs Little began to cry. 'My poor dear little son!' she said. 'I know he'll get wedged somewhere.'

'Just because *you* can't travel comfortably in a mousehole doesn't mean that it isn't a perfectly suitable place for Stuart,' said Mr Little. 'Just don't get yourself all worked up.'

'Maybe we ought to lower some food to him,' suggested George. 'That's what the State Police did when a man got stuck in a cave.' George darted into the kitchen and came running back with a dish of applesauce. 'We can pour some of this in, and it will run down to where he is.' George spooned out a bit of the applesauce and started to poke it into the hole.

'Stop that!' bellowed Mr Little. 'George, will you kindly let *me* handle this situation? Put that applesauce away immediately!'

Mr Little glared fiercely at George.

'I was just trying to help my own brother,' said George, shaking his head as he carried the sauce back to the kitchen.

'Let's all call to Stuart,' suggested Mrs Little. 'It is quite possible that the mousehole branches and twists about, and that he has lost his way.'

'Very well,' said Mr Little. 'I will count three, then we will all call, then we will all keep perfectly quiet for three seconds, listening for the answer.' He took out his watch.

Mr and Mrs Little and George got down on their hands and knees and put their mouths as close as possible to the mousehole. Then they all called: 'Stooooo-art!' And then they all kept perfectly still for three seconds.

Stuart, from his cramped position inside the rolled-up shade, heard them yelling in the pantry and called back, 'Here I am!' But he had such a weak voice and was so far inside

the shade that the other members of the family
did not hear his answering cry.

'Again!' said Mr Little. 'One, two, three –
Stooooo-art!'

It was no use. No answer was heard. Mrs
Little went up to her bedroom, lay down, and
sobbed. Mr Little went to the telephone and
called up the Bureau of Missing Persons,
but when the man asked for a description
of Stuart and was told that he was only two
inches high, he hung up in disgust. George
meantime went down to the cellar and hunted

around to see if he could find the other entrance to the mousehole. He moved a great many trunks, suitcases, flowerpots, baskets, boxes, and broken chairs from one end of the cellar to the other in order to get at the section of wall which he thought was likeliest, but found no hole. He did, however, come across an old discarded rowing machine of Mr Little's, and becoming interested in this, carried it upstairs with some difficulty and spent the rest of the morning rowing.

When lunchtime came (everybody had forgotten about breakfast) all three sat down to a lamb stew which Mrs Little had prepared, but it was a sad meal, each one trying not to stare at the small empty chair which Stuart always occupied, right next to Mrs Little's glass of water. No one could eat, so great was the sorrow. George ate a bit of dessert but nothing else. When lunch was over Mrs Little broke out crying again, and said she thought Stuart must be dead. 'Nonsense, nonsense!' growled Mr Little.

'If he *is* dead,' said George, 'we ought to pull down the shades all through the house.' And he raced to the windows and began pulling down the shades.

'George!' shouted Mr Little in an exasperated tone, 'if you don't stop acting in an idiotic fashion, I will have to punish you. We are having enough trouble today without having to cope with your foolishness.'

But George had already run into the living room and had begun to darken it, to show his respect for the dead. He pulled a cord and out dropped Stuart on to the windowsill.

'Well, for the love of Pete,' said George. 'Look who's here, Mom!'

'It's about time somebody pulled down that shade,' remarked Stuart. 'That's all I can say.' He was quite weak and hungry.

Mrs Little was so overjoyed to see him that she kept right on crying. Of course, everybody wanted to know how it had happened.

'It was simply an accident that might happen to anybody,' said Stuart. 'As for my hat and cane being found at the entrance to the mousehole, you can draw your own conclusions.'

6. A Fair Breeze

ONE morning when the wind was from the west, Stuart put on his sailor suit and his sailor hat, took his spyglass down from the shelf, and set out for a walk, full of the joy of life and the fear of dogs. With a rolling gait he sauntered along toward Fifth Avenue, keeping a sharp lookout.

Whenever he spied a dog through his glass, Stuart would hurry to the nearest doorman, climb his trouserleg, and hide in the tails of his uniform. And once, when no doorman

was handy, he had to crawl into a yesterday's paper and roll himself up in the second section till danger was past.

At the corner of Fifth Avenue there were several people waiting for the uptown bus, and Stuart joined them. Nobody noticed him, because he wasn't tall enough to be noticed.

'I'm not tall enough to be noticed,' thought Stuart, 'yet I'm tall enough to want to go to Seventy-second Street.'

When the bus came into view, all the men waved their canes and briefcases at the driver, and Stuart waved his spyglass. Then, knowing that the step of the bus would be too high for him, Stuart seized hold of the cuff of a gentleman's pants and was swung aboard without any trouble or inconvenience whatever.

Stuart never paid any fare on buses, because he wasn't big enough to carry an ordinary dime. The only time he had ever attempted to carry a dime, he had rolled the coin along like

a hoop while he raced along beside it; but it had got away from him on a hill and had been snatched up by an old woman with no teeth. After that experience Stuart contented himself with the tiny coins which his father made for him out of tin foil. They were handsome little things, although rather hard to see without putting on your spectacles.

When the conductor came around to collect the fares, Stuart fished in his purse and pulled out a coin no bigger than the eye of a grasshopper.

'What's that you're offering me?' asked the conductor.

'It's one of my dimes,' said Stuart.

'Is it, now?' said the conductor. 'Well, I'd have a fine time explaining that to the bus company. Why, you're no bigger than a dime yourself.'

'Yes I am,' replied Stuart angrily. 'I'm more than twice as big as a dime. A dime only comes up to here on me.' And Stuart pointed to his hip. 'Furthermore,' he added, 'I didn't come on this bus to be insulted.'

'I beg pardon,' said the conductor. 'You'll have to forgive me, for I had no idea that in all the world there was such a small sailor.'

'Live and learn,' muttered Stuart, tartly, putting his change purse back in his pocket.

When the bus stopped at Seventy-second Street, Stuart jumped out and hurried across to the sailboat pond in Central Park. Over the pond the west wind blew, and into the teeth of the west wind sailed the sloops and

schooners, their rails well down, their wet
decks gleaming. The owners, boys and grown
men, raced around the cement shores hoping
to arrive at the other side in time to keep the
boats from bumping. Some of the toy boats
were not as small as you might think, for
when you got close to them you found that
their mainmast was taller than a man's head,
and they were beautifully made, with
everything shipshape and ready for sea. To
Stuart they seemed enormous, and he hoped
he would be able to get aboard one of them

and sail away to the far corners of the pond. (He was an adventurous little fellow and loved the feel of the breeze in his face and the cry of the gulls overhead and the heave of the great swell under him.)

As he sat cross-legged on the wall that surrounds the pond, gazing out at the ships through his spyglass, Stuart noticed one boat that seemed to him finer and prouder than any other. Her name was *Wasp*. She was a big, black schooner flying the American flag. She had a clipper bow, and on her foredeck was mounted a three-inch cannon. She's the ship for me, thought Stuart. And the next time she

sailed in, he ran over to where she was being turned around.

'Excuse me, sir,' said Stuart to the man who was turning her, 'but are you the owner of the schooner *Wasp*?'

'I am,' replied the man, surprised to be addressed by a mouse in a sailor suit.

'I'm looking for a berth in a good ship,' continued Stuart, 'and I thought perhaps you might sign me on. I'm strong and I'm quick.'

'Are you sober?' asked the owner of the *Wasp*.

'I do my work,' said Stuart, crisply.

The man looked sharply at him. He couldn't help admiring the trim appearance and bold manner of this diminutive seafaring character.

'Well,' he said at length, pointing the prow of the *Wasp* out toward the centre of the pond, 'I'll tell you what I'll do with you. You see that big racing sloop out there?'

'I do,' said Stuart.

'That's the *Lillian B. Womrath*,' said the man, 'and I hate her with all my heart.'

'Then so do I,' cried Stuart, loyally.

'I hate her because she is always bumping into my boat,' continued the man, 'and because her owner is a lazy boy who doesn't understand sailing and who hardly knows a squall from a squid.'

'Or a jib from a jibe,' cried Stuart.

'Or a luff from a leech,' bellowed the man.

'Or a deck from a dock,' screamed Stuart.

'Or a mast from a mist,' yelled the man. 'But hold on, now, no more of this! I'll tell you what we'll do. The *Lillian B. Womrath* has always been able to beat the *Wasp* sailing, but I believe that if my schooner were properly handled it would be a different story. Nobody knows how I suffer, standing here on shore, helpless, watching the *Wasp* blunder along, when all she needs is a steady hand on her helm. So, my young friend, I'll let you sail the *Wasp* across the pond and back, and if you can beat that detestable sloop I'll give you a regular job.'

'Aye, aye, sir!' said Stuart, swinging himself aboard the schooner and taking his place at the wheel. 'Ready about!'

'One moment,' said the man. 'Do you mind telling me *how* you propose to beat the other boat?'

'I intend to crack on more sail,' said Stuart.

'Not in *my* boat, thank you,' replied the man quickly. 'I don't want you capsizing in a squall.'

'Well, then,' said Stuart, 'I'll catch the sloop broad on, and rake her with fire from my forward gun.'

'Foul means!' said the man. 'I want this to be a boat race, not a naval engagement.'

'Well, then,' said Stuart cheerfully, 'I'll sail the *Wasp* straight and true, and let the *Lillian B. Womrath* go yawing all over the pond.'

'Bravo!' cried the man, 'and good luck go with you!' And so saying, he let go of the *Wasp*'s prow. A puff of air bellied out the schooner's headsails and she paid off and filled away on the port tack, heeling gracefully over to the breeze while Stuart twirled her wheel and braced himself against a deck cleat.

'By the by,' yelled the man, 'you haven't told me your name.'

'Name is Stuart Little,' called Stuart at the top of his lungs. 'I'm the second son of Frederick C. Little, of this city.'

'*Bon voyage*, Stuart,' hollered his friend, 'take care of yourself and bring the *Wasp* home safe.'

'That I will,' shouted Stuart. And he was so proud and happy, he let go of the wheel for a second and did a little dance on the sloping

deck, never noticing how narrowly he escaped hitting a tramp steamer that was drifting in his path, with her engines disabled and her decks awash.

7. The Sailboat Race

WHEN the people in Central Park learned that one of the toy sailboats was being steered by a mouse in a sailor suit, they all came running. Soon the shores of the pond were so crowded that a policeman was sent from headquarters to announce that

everybody would have to stop pushing, but nobody did. People in New York like to push each other. The most excited person of all was the boy who owned the *Lillian B. Womrath*. He was a fat, sulky boy of twelve, named LeRoy. He wore a blue serge suit and a white necktie stained with orange juice.

'Come back here!' he called to Stuart. 'Come back here and get on *my* boat. I want you to steer *my* boat. I will pay you five dollars a week and you can have every Thursday afternoon off and a radio in your room.'

'I thank you for your kind offer,' replied Stuart, 'but I am happy aboard the *Wasp* – happier than I have ever been before in all my life.' And with that he spun the wheel over smartly and headed his schooner down toward the starting line, where LeRoy was turning his boat around by poking it with a long stick, ready for the start of the race.

'I'll be the referee,' said a man in a bright green suit. 'Is the *Wasp* ready?'

'Ready, sir!' shouted Stuart, touching his hat.

'Is the *Lillian B. Womrath* ready?' asked the referee.

'Sure, I'm ready,' said LeRoy.

'To the north end of the pond and back again!' shouted the referee. 'On your mark, get set, GO!'

'Go!' cried the people along the shore.

'Go!' cried the owner of the *Wasp*.

'Go!' yelled the policeman.

And away went the two boats for the north end of the pond, while the seagulls wheeled and cried overhead and the taxicabs tooted and honked from Seventy-second Street and the west wind (which had come halfway across America to get to Central Park) sang and whistled in the rigging and blew spray across the decks, stinging Stuart's cheeks with tiny fragments of flying peanut shell tossed up from the foamy deep. 'This is the life for me!' Stuart murmured to himself. 'What a ship! What a day! What a race!'

Before the two boats had gone many feet, however, an accident happened on shore. The people were pushing each other harder and harder in their eagerness to see the sport, and although they really didn't mean to, they pushed the policeman so hard they pushed him right off the concrete wall and into the pond. He hit the water in a sitting position, and got wet clear up to the third button of his jacket. He was soaked.

This particular policeman was not only a big, heavy man, but he had just eaten a big, heavy meal, and the wave he made went curling outward, cresting and billowing, upsetting all manner of small craft and causing every owner of a boat on the pond to scream with delight and consternation.

When Stuart saw the great wave approaching he jumped for the rigging, but he was too late. Towering above the *Wasp* like a mountain,

the wave came crashing and piling along the deck, caught Stuart up and swept him over the side and into the water, where everybody supposed he would drown. Stuart had no intention of drowning. He kicked hard with his feet, and thrashed hard with his tail, and in a minute or two he climbed back aboard the schooner, cold and wet but quite unharmed. As he took his place at the helm, he could hear people cheering for him and calling, 'Atta

mouse, Stuart! Atta mouse!' He looked over and saw that the wave had capsized the *Lillian B. Womrath* but that she had righted herself and was sailing on her course, close by. And she stayed close alongside till both boats reached the north end of the pond. Here Stuart put the *Wasp* about and LeRoy turned the *Lillian* around with his stick, and away the two boats went for the finish line.

'This race isn't over yet,' thought Stuart.

The first warning he had that there was trouble ahead came when he glanced into the *Wasp*'s cabin and observed that the barometer had fallen sharply. That can mean only one thing at sea – dirty weather. Suddenly a dark cloud swept across the sun, blotting it out and leaving the earth in shadow. Stuart shivered in his wet clothes. He turned up his sailor blouse closer around his neck, and when he spied the *Wasp*'s owner among the crowd on shore he waved his hat and called out:

'Dirty weather ahead, sir! Wind backing into the south-west, seas confused, glass falling.'

'Never mind the weather!' cried the owner. 'Watch out for flotsam dead ahead!'

Stuart peered ahead into the gathering storm, but saw nothing except grey waves with white crests. The world seemed cold and ominous. Stuart glanced behind him. There came the sloop, boiling along fast, rolling up a bow wave and gaining steadily.

'Look out, Stuart! Look out where you're going!'

Stuart strained his eyes, and suddenly, dead ahead, right in the path of the *Wasp*, he saw an enormous paper bag looming up on the surface of the pond. The bag was empty and riding high, its open end gaping wide like the mouth of a cave. Stuart spun the wheel over but it was too late: the *Wasp* drove her bowsprit straight into the bag and with a fearful *whooosh* the schooner slowed down and came up into the wind with all sails

flapping. Just at this moment Stuart heard a splintering crash, saw the bow of the *Lillian* plough through his rigging, and felt the whole ship tremble from stem to stern with the force of the collision.

'A collision!' shouted the crowd on shore.

In a jiffy the two boats were in a terrible tangle. Little boys on shore screamed and danced up and down. Meanwhile the paper bag sprang a leak and began to fill.

The *Wasp* couldn't move because of the bag. The *Lillian B. Womrath* couldn't move because her nose was stuck in the *Wasp*'s rigging.

Waving his arms, Stuart ran forward and fired off his gun. Then he heard, above the other voices on shore, the voice of the owner of the *Wasp* yelling directions and telling him what to do.

'Stuart! Stuart! Down jib! Down staysail!'

Stuart jumped for the halyards, and the jib and the forestaysail came rippling down.

'Cut away all paper bags!' roared the owner.

Stuart whipped out his pocketknife and slashed away bravely at the soggy bag until he had the deck cleared.

'Now back your foresail and give her a full!' screamed the owner of the *Wasp*.

Stuart grabbed the foresail boom and pulled with all his might. Slowly the schooner paid off and began to gather headway. And as she heeled over to the breeze she rolled her rail out from under the *Lillian*'s nose, shook herself free, and stood away to the southard. A loud cheer went up from the bank. Stuart sprang to the wheel and answered it. Then he looked back, and to his great joy he perceived that the *Lillian* had gone off in a wild direction and was yawing all over the pond.

Straight and true sailed the *Wasp*, with Stuart at the helm. After she had crossed the finish line, Stuart brought her alongside the wall, and was taken ashore and highly praised for his fine seamanship and daring. The owner was delighted and said it was the happiest day of his life. He introduced himself to Stuart, said that in private life he was Dr Paul Carey,

a surgeon-dentist. He said model boats were his hobby and that he would be delighted to have Stuart take command of his vessel at any time. Everybody shook hands with Stuart –

everybody, that is, except the policeman, who was too wet and mad to shake hands with a mouse.

When Stuart got home that night, his brother George asked him where he had been all day.

'Oh, knocking around town,' replied Stuart.

8. Margalo

BECAUSE he was so small, Stuart was often hard to find around the house. His father and his mother and his brother George seldom could locate him by looking for him – usually they had to call him; and the house often echoed with cries of 'Stuart! Stooo-art!' You would come into a room, and he might be curled up in a chair, but you wouldn't see him. Mr Little was in constant fear of losing him and never finding him again. He even made him a tiny red cap, such as hunters wear, so that he would be easier to see.

One day when he was seven years old, Stuart was in the kitchen watching his mother make tapioca pudding. He was feeling hungry, and when Mrs Little opened the door of the electric refrigerator to get something, Stuart slipped inside to see if he could find a piece of cheese. He supposed, of course, his mother had seen him, and when the door swung shut and he realized he was locked in, it surprised him greatly.

'Help!' he called. 'It's dark in here. It's cold in this refrigerator. Help! Let me out! I'm getting colder by the minute.'

But his voice was not strong enough to penetrate the thick wall. In the darkness he stumbled and fell into a saucer of prunes. The juice was cold. Stuart shivered, and his teeth chattered together. It wasn't until half an hour later that Mrs Little again opened the door and found him standing on a butter plate, beating his arms together to try to keep warm, and blowing on his hands, and hopping up and down.

'Mercy!' she cried. 'Stuart, my poor little boy.'

'How about a nip of brandy?' said Stuart. 'I'm chilled to the bone.'

But his mother made him some hot broth instead, and put him to bed in his cigarette box with a doll's hot-water bottle against his feet. Even so, Stuart caught a bad cold, and this turned into bronchitis, and Stuart had to stay in bed for almost two weeks.

During his illness, the other members of the family were extremely kind to Stuart. Mrs Little played tick-tack-toe with him. George

made him a soap bubble pipe and a bow and arrow. Mr Little made him a pair of ice skates out of two paper clips.

One cold afternoon Mrs Little was shaking her dustcloth out of the window when she noticed a small bird lying on the windowsill, apparently dead. She brought it in and put it near the radiator, and in a short while it fluttered its wings and opened its eyes. It was a pretty little hen-bird, brown, with a streak of yellow on her breast. The Littles didn't agree on what kind of bird she was.

'She's a wall-eyed vireo,' said George, scientifically.

'I think she's more like a young wren,' said Mr Little. Anyway, they fixed a place for her in the living room, and fed her, and gave her a cup of water. Soon she felt much better and went hopping around the house, examining everything with the greatest care and interest. Presently she hopped upstairs and into Stuart's room where he was lying in bed.

'Hello,' said Stuart. 'Who are you? Where did you come from?'

'My name is Margalo,' said the bird, softly, in a musical voice. 'I come from fields once tall with wheat, from pastures deep in fern and thistle; I come from vales of meadowsweet, and I love to whistle.'

Stuart sat bolt upright in bed. 'Say that again!' he said.

'I can't,' replied Margalo. 'I have a sore throat.'

'So have I,' said Stuart. 'I've got bronchitis. You better not get too near me, you might catch it.'

'I'll stay right here by the door,' said Margalo.

'You can use some of my gargle if you want to,' said Stuart. 'And here are some nose drops, and I have plenty of Kleenex.'

'Thank you very much, you are very kind,' replied the bird.

'Did they take your temperature?' asked Stuart, who was beginning to be genuinely worried about his new friend's health.

'No,' said Margalo, 'but I don't think it will be necessary.'

'Well, we better make sure,' said Stuart, 'because I would hate to have anything happen to you. Here ...' And he tossed her the thermometer. Margalo put it under her tongue,

and she and Stuart sat very still for three
minutes. Then she took it out and looked at it,
turning it slowly and carefully.

'Normal,' she announced. Stuart felt his
heart leap for gladness. It seemed to him that
he had never seen any creature so beautiful as
this tiny bird, and he already loved her.

'I hope,' he remarked, 'that my parents have
fixed you up with a decent place to sleep.'

'Oh, yes,' Margalo replied. 'I'm going to
sleep in the Boston fern on the bookshelf in the

living room. It's a nice place, for a city location. And now, if you'll excuse me, I think I shall go to bed – I see it's getting dark outside. I always go to bed at sundown. Good night, sir!'

'Please don't call me "sir,"' cried Stuart. 'Call me Stuart.'

'Very well,' said the bird. 'Good night, Stuart!' And she hopped off, with light, bouncing steps.

'Good night, Margalo,' called Stuart. 'See you in the morning.'

Stuart settled back under the bedclothes again. 'There's a mighty fine bird,' he whispered, and sighed a tender sigh.

When Mrs Little came in, later, to tuck Stuart in for the night and hear his prayers, Stuart asked her if she thought the bird would be quite safe sleeping down in the living room.

'Quite safe, my dear,' replied Mrs Little.

'What about that cat Snowbell?' asked Stuart, sternly.

'Snowbell won't touch the bird,' his mother said. 'You go to sleep and forget all about it.'

Mrs Little opened the window and turned out the light.

Stuart closed his eyes and lay there in the dark, but he couldn't seem to go to sleep. He tossed and turned, and the bedclothes got all rumpled up. He kept thinking about the bird downstairs asleep in the fern. He kept thinking about Snowbell and about the way Snowbell's eyes gleamed. Finally, unable to stand it any longer, he switched on the light. 'There's just something in me that doesn't trust a cat,' he muttered. 'I can't sleep, knowing that Margalo is in danger.'

Pushing the covers back, Stuart climbed out of bed. He put on his wrapper and slippers. Taking his bow and arrow and his flashlight, he tiptoed out into the hall. Everybody had gone to bed and the house was dark. Stuart found his way to the stairs and descended slowly and cautiously into the living room, making no noise. His throat hurt him, and he felt a little bit dizzy.

'Sick as I am,' he said to himself, 'this has got to be done.'

Being careful not to make a sound, he stole across to the lamp by the bookshelf, shinnied up the cord, and climbed out on to the shelf. There was a faint ray of light from the street lamp outside, and Stuart could dimly see Margalo, asleep in the fern, her head tucked under her wing.

'Sleep dwell upon thine eyes, peace in thy breast,' he whispered, repeating a speech he had heard in the movies. Then he hid behind a candlestick and waited, listening and watching. For half an hour he saw nothing, heard nothing but the faint ruffle of Margalo's wings when she stirred in dream. The clock struck ten, loudly, and before the sound of the last stroke had died away Stuart saw two gleaming yellow eyes peering out from behind the sofa.

'So!' thought Stuart. 'I guess there's going to be something doing after all.' He reached for his bow and arrow.

The eyes came nearer. Stuart was frightened, but he was a brave mouse, even when he had a sore throat. He placed the arrow against the cord of the bow and waited. Snowbell crept softly toward the bookshelf and climbed noiselessly up into the chair within easy reach of the Boston fern where Margalo was asleep. Then he crouched, ready to spring. His tail waved back and forth. His eyes gleamed bright. Stuart decided the time had come. He stepped out from behind the candlestick, knelt down, bent his bow, and took careful aim at Snowbell's left ear – which was the nearest to him.

'This is the finest thing I have ever done,' thought Stuart. And he shot the arrow straight into the cat's ear.

Snowbell squealed with pain and jumped down and ran off toward the kitchen.

'A direct hit!' said Stuart. 'Thank heaven! Well, there's a good night's work done.' And

he threw a kiss toward Margalo's sleeping form.

It was a tired little mouse that crawled into bed a few minutes later – tired but ready for sleep at last.

9. A Narrow Escape

MARGALO liked it so well at the Littles' house she decided to stay for a while instead of returning to the open country. She and Stuart became fast friends, and as the days passed it seemed to Stuart that she grew more and more beautiful. He hoped she would never go away from him.

One day when Stuart had recovered from bronchitis he took his new skates and put on his ski pants and went out to look for an ice pond. He didn't get far. The minute he stepped out into the street he saw an Irish terrier, so he

had to shinny up an iron gate and jump into a garbage can, where he hid in a grove of celery.

While he was there, waiting for the dog to go away, a garbage truck from the Department of Sanitation drove up to the curb and two men picked up the can. Stuart felt himself being hoisted high in the air. He peered over the side and saw that in another instant he and everything in the can would be dumped into the big truck.

'If I jump now I'll kill myself,' thought Stuart. So he ducked back into the can and waited. The men threw the can with a loud bump into the truck, where another man grabbed it, turned it upside down, and shook everything out. Stuart landed on his head, buried two feet deep in wet slippery garbage.

All around him was garbage, smelling strong. Under him, over him, on all four sides of him – garbage. Just an enormous world of garbage and trash and smell. It was a messy spot to be in. He had egg on his trousers, butter on his cap, gravy on his shirt, orange pulp in his ear, and banana peel wrapped around his waist.

Still hanging on to his skates, Stuart tried to make his way up to the surface of the garbage, but the footing was bad. He climbed a pile of coffee grounds, but near the top the grounds gave way under him and he slid down and landed in a pool of leftover rice pudding.

'I bet I'm going to be sick at my stomach before I get out of this,' said Stuart.

He was anxious to work his way up to the top of the pile because he was afraid of being squashed by the next can-load of garbage. When at last he did succeed in getting to the surface, tired and smelly, he observed that the truck was not making any more collections but was rumbling rapidly along. Stuart glanced up at the sun. 'We're going east,' he said to himself. 'I wonder what that means.'

There was no way for him to get out of the truck, the sides were too high. He just had to wait.

When the truck arrived at the East River, which borders New York City on the east and which is a rather dirty but useful river, the

driver drove out on to the pier, backed up to a garbage scow, and dumped his load. Stuart went crashing and slithering along with everything else and hit his head so hard he fainted and lay quite still, as though dead. He lay that way for almost an hour, and when he recovered his senses he looked about him and saw nothing but water. The scow was being towed out to sea.

'Well,' thought Stuart, 'this is about the worst thing that could happen to anybody. I guess this will be my last ride in *this* world.' For he knew that the garbage would be towed twenty miles out and dumped into the Atlantic

Ocean. 'I guess there's nothing I can do about it,' he thought, hopelessly. 'I'll just have to sit here bravely and die like a man. But I wish I didn't have to die with egg on my pants and butter on my cap and gravy on my shirt and orange pulp in my ear and banana peel wrapped around my middle.'

The thought of death made Stuart sad, and he began to think of his home and of his father and mother and brother and of Margalo and Snowbell and of how he loved them (all but Snowbell) and of what a pleasant place his home was, specially in the early morning with the light just coming in through the curtains and the household stirring and waking. The tears came into his eyes when he realized that he would never see them again. He was still sobbing when a small voice behind him whispered:

'Stuart!'

He looked around, through his tears, and there, sitting on a Brussels sprout, was Margalo.

'Margalo!' cried Stuart. 'How did *you* get here?'

'Well,' said the bird, 'I was looking out the window this morning when you left home and I happened to see you get dumped into the garbage truck, so I flew out the window and followed the truck, thinking you might need help.'

'I've never been so glad to see anybody in all my life,' said Stuart. 'But how are you going to help me?'

'I think that if you'll hang on to my feet,' said Margalo, 'I can fly ashore with you. It's worth trying anyway. How much do you weigh?'

'Three ounces and a half,' said Stuart.

'With your clothes on?' asked Margalo.

'Certainly,' replied Stuart, modestly.

'Then I believe I can carry you all right.'

'Suppose I get dizzy,' said Stuart.

'Don't look down,' replied Margalo. 'Then you won't get dizzy.'

'Suppose I get sick at my stomach.'

'You'll just have to *be* sick,' the bird replied. 'Anything is better than death.'

'Yes, that's true,' Stuart agreed.

'Hang on, then! We may as well get started.'

Stuart tucked his skates into his shirt, stepped gingerly on to a tuft of lettuce, and took a firm grip on Margalo's ankles. 'All ready!' he cried.

With a flutter of wings, Margalo rose into the sky, carrying Stuart along, and together

they flew out over the ocean and headed
toward home.

'Pew!' said Margalo, when they were high
in the air, 'you smell awful, Stuart.'

'I know I do,' he replied, gloomily. 'I hope it
isn't making you feel bad.'

'I can hardly breathe,' she answered. 'And
my heart is pounding in my breast. Isn't there
something you could drop to make yourself
lighter?'

'Well, I could drop these ice skates,' said Stuart.

'Goodness me,' the little bird cried, 'I didn't know you had skates hidden in your shirt. Toss those heavy skates away quickly or we will both come down in the ocean and perish.' Stuart threw his skates away and watched them fall down, down, till they disappeared in the grey waves below. 'That's better,' said Margalo. 'Now we're all right. I can already see the towers and chimneys of New York.'

Fifteen minutes later, in they flew through the open window of the Littles' living room and landed on the Boston fern. Mrs Little, who had left the window up when she missed

Margalo, was glad to see them back, for she was beginning to worry. When she heard what had happened and how near she had come to losing her son, she took Stuart in her hand, even though his clothes smelled nasty, and kissed him. Then she sent him upstairs to take a bath, and sent George out to take Stuart's clothes to the cleaner.

'What was it like, out there in the Atlantic Ocean?' inquired Mr Little, who had never been very far from home.

So Stuart and Margalo told all about the ocean, and the grey waves curling with white crests, and the gulls in the sky, and the channel buoys and the ships and the tugs and the wind making a sound in your ears. Mr Little sighed and said some day he hoped to get away from business long enough to see all those fine things.

Everyone thanked Margalo for saving Stuart's life; and at suppertime Mrs Little presented her with a tiny cake, which had seeds sprinkled on top.

10. Springtime

SNOWBELL, the cat, enjoyed nighttime more than daytime. Perhaps it was because his eyes liked the dark. But I think it was because there are always so many worthwhile things going on in New York at night.

Snowbell had several friends in the neighborhood. Some of them were house cats, others were store cats. He knew a Maltese cat in the A & P, a white Persian in the apartment house next door, a tortoiseshell in the delicatessen, a tiger cat in the basement of the branch library, and a beautiful young Angora who had escaped from a cage in a pet shop on Third Avenue and had gone to live a free life of her own in the tool house of the small park near Stuart's home.

One fine spring evening Snowbell had been calling on the Angora in the park. He started home, late, and it was such a lovely night she said she would walk along with him to keep him company. When they got to Mr Little's house, the two cats sat down at the foot of a tall vine which ran up the side of the house past George's bedroom. This vine was useful to Snowbell, because he could climb it at night and crawl into the house through George's open window. Snowbell began telling his friend about Margalo and Stuart.

'Goodness,' said the Angora cat, 'you mean to say you live in the same house with a bird and a mouse and don't do anything about it?'

'That's the situation,' replied Snowbell. 'But what can I do about it? Please remember that

Stuart is a member of the family, and the bird is a permanent guest, like myself.'

'Well,' said Snowbell's friend, 'all I can say is, you've got more self-control than I have.'

'Doubtless,' said Snowbell. 'However, I sometimes think I've got too much self-control for my own good. I've been terribly nervous and upset lately, and I think it's because I'm always holding myself in.'

The cats' voices grew louder, and they talked so loudly that they never heard a slight rustling in the vine a few feet above their heads. It was a grey pigeon, who had been asleep there and who had awakened at the sound of cats and begun to listen. 'This sounds like an interesting conversation,' said the pigeon to himself. 'Maybe I'd better stay around and see if I can learn something.'

'Look here,' he heard the Angora cat say to Snowbell, 'I admit that a cat has a duty toward her own people, and that under the circumstances it would be wrong for you to eat Margalo. But *I'm* not a member of your family and there is nothing to stop *me* from eating her, is there?'

'Nothing that I can think of offhand,' said Snowbell.

'Then here I go,' said the Angora, starting up the vine. The pigeon was wide awake by this time, ready to fly away; but the voices down below continued.

'Wait a minute,' said Snowbell, 'don't be in such a hurry. I don't think you'd better go in there tonight.'

'Why not?' asked the other cat.

'Well, for one thing, you're not supposed to enter our house. It's unlawful entry, and you might get into trouble.'

'I won't get into any trouble,' said the Angora.

'Please wait till tomorrow night,' said Snowbell, firmly. 'Mr and Mrs Little will be going out tomorrow night, and you won't be taking such a risk. It's for your own good I'm suggesting this.'

'Oh, all right,' agreed the Angora. 'I guess I can wait. But tell me where I'll find the bird, after I do get in.'

'That's simple,' said Snowbell. 'Climb this vine, enter George's room through the open window, then go downstairs and you'll find the bird asleep in the Boston fern on the bookcase.'

'Easy enough,' said the Angora, licking her chops. 'I'm obliged to you, sir.'

'Well, the old thing!' whispered the pigeon to himself, and he flew away quickly to find a piece of writing paper and a pencil. Snowbell said goodnight to his friend and climbed up the vine and went in to bed.

Next morning Margalo found a note on the branch of her fern when she woke. It said: BEWARE OF A STRANGE CAT WHO WILL COME BY NIGHT. It was signed A WELL WISHER. She kept the note under her wing all day long, wondering what she had better do, but she didn't dare show it to anyone – not even to Stuart. She couldn't eat, she was so frightened.

'What had I better do?' she kept saying to herself.

Finally, just before dark, she hopped up to an open window and without saying anything to anybody she flew away. It was springtime, and she flew north, just as fast as she could fly, because something inside her told her that north was the way for a bird to go when spring comes to the land.

11. The Automobile

FOR THREE days everybody hunted all over the house for Margalo without finding so much as a feather.

'I guess she had spring fever,' said George. 'A normal bird doesn't stay indoors this kind of weather.'

'Perhaps she has a husband somewhere and has gone to meet him,' suggested Mr Little.

'She has not!' sobbed Stuart, bitterly. 'That's just a lot of nonsense.'

'How do *you* know?' asked George.

'Because I asked her one time,' cried Stuart. 'She told me she was a single bird.'

Everybody questioned Snowbell closely, but the cat insisted he knew nothing about Margalo's disappearance. 'I don't see why you have to make a pariah out of me just because that disagreeable little chippy flew the coop,' said Snowbell, irritably.

Stuart was heartbroken. He had no appetite, refused food, and lost weight. Finally he decided that he would run away from home without telling anybody, and go out into the world and look for Margalo. 'While I am about it, I might as well seek my fortune, too,' he thought.

Before daybreak next morning he got out his biggest handkerchief and in it he placed his toothbrush, his money, his soap, his comb and brush, a clean suit of underwear, and his pocket compass.

'I ought to take along something to remember my mother by,' he thought. So he crept into his mother's bedroom where she was still asleep, climbed the lamp cord to her bureau, and pulled a strand of Mrs Little's hair from her comb. He rolled the hair up neatly and laid it in the handkerchief with the other things. Then he rolled everything up into a bundle and tied it on to one end of a wooden match. With his grey felt hat cocked jauntily on one side of his head and his pack slung across his shoulder, Stuart stole softly out of the house.

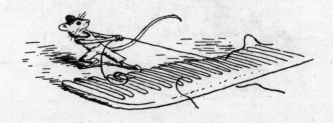

'Goodbye, beautiful home,' he whispered. 'I wonder if I will ever see you again.'

Stuart stood uncertainly for a moment in the street in front of the house. The world was a big place in which to go looking for a lost bird. North, south, east, or west – which way should he *go*? Stuart decided that he needed advice on such an important matter, so he started uptown to find his friend Dr Carey, the surgeon-dentist, owner of the schooner *Wasp*.

The doctor was glad to see Stuart. He took him right into his inner office where he was busy pulling a man's tooth. The man's name was Edward Clydesdale, and he had several wads of gauze in his cheek to hold his mouth open good and wide. The tooth was a hard one to get out, and the Doctor let Stuart sit on his instrument tray so they could talk during the operation.

'This is my friend, Stuart Little,' he said to the man with the gauze in his cheek.

'How 'oo oo, Soo'rt,' replied the man, as best he could.

'Very well, thank you,' replied Stuart.

'Well, what's on your mind, Stuart?' asked Dr Carey, seizing hold of the man's tooth with a pair of pincers and giving a strong pull.

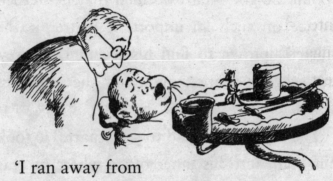

'I ran away from home this morning,' explained Stuart. 'I am going out into the world to seek my fortune and to look for a lost bird. Which direction do you think I should start out in?'

Dr Carey twisted the tooth a bit and racked it back and forth. 'What colour is the bird?' he asked.

'Brown,' said Stuart.

'Better go north,' said Dr Carey. 'Don't you think so, Mr Clydesdale?'

' 'ook in 'entral 'ark,' said Mr Clydesdale.

'What?' cried Stuart.

'I 'ay, 'ook in 'entral 'ark,' said Mr Clydesdale.

'He says look in Central Park,' explained Dr Carey, tucking another big wad of gauze into Mr Clydesdale's cheek. 'And it's a good suggestion. Oftentimes people with decayed teeth have sound ideas. Central Park is a favourite place for birds in the spring.' Mr Clydesdale was nodding his head vigorously, and seemed about to speak again.

'If 'oo 'on't 'ocate a 'ird in 'entral 'ark, 'ake a 'ew 'ork 'ew 'aven & 'artford 'ailway 'n 'ook in 'onnecticut.'

'What?' cried Stuart, delighted at this new kind of talk. 'What say, Mr Clydesdale?'

'If 'oo 'on't 'ocate a 'ird in 'entral 'ark, 'ake a 'ew 'ork 'ew 'aven & 'artford' 'ailway 'n 'ook in 'onnecticut.'

'He says if you can't locate the bird in Central Park, take a New York New Haven & Hartford Railway train and look in Connecticut,' said Dr Carey. Then he removed the rolls of gauze from Mr Clydesdale's mouth. 'Rinse, please!' he said.

Mr Clydesdale took a glass of mouthwash that was beside the chair and rinsed his mouth out.

'Tell me this, Stuart,' said Dr Carey. 'How are you travelling? On foot?'

'Yes, sir,' said Stuart.

'Well, I think you'd better have a car. As soon as I get this tooth out, we'll see what can be done about it. Open, please, Mr Clydesdale.'

Dr Carey grabbed the tooth with the pincers again, and this time he pulled so long and so hard and with such determination that the tooth popped out, which was a great relief to everybody, particularly to Mr Clydesdale. The Doctor then led Stuart into another room. From a shelf he took a tiny automobile, about

six inches long – the most perfect miniature automobile Stuart had ever seen. It was bright yellow with black fenders, a streamlined car of graceful design. 'I made this myself,' Dr Carey said. 'I enjoy building model cars and boats and other things when I am not extracting teeth. This car has a real gasoline motor in it. It has quite a good deal of power – do you think you can handle it, Stuart?'

'Certainly,' replied Stuart, looking into the driver's seat and blowing the horn. 'But isn't it going to attract too much attention? Won't everybody stop and stare at such a small automobile?'

'They would if they could see you,' replied Dr Carey, 'but nobody will be able to see you, or the car.'

'Why not?' asked Stuart.

'Because this automobile is a thoroughly modern car. It's not only noiseless, it's invisible. Nobody can see it.'

'*I* can see it,' remarked Stuart.

'Push that little button!' said the Doctor, pointing to a button on the instrument panel. Stuart pushed the button. Instantly the car vanished from sight.

'Now push it again,' said the Doctor.

'How can I push it when I can't see it?' asked Stuart.

'Feel around for it.'

So Stuart felt around until his hand came in contact with a button. It seemed like the same button, and Stuart pushed it. He heard a slight grinding noise and felt something slip out from under his hand.

'Hey, watch out!' yelled Dr Carey. 'You pushed the starter button. She's off! There she goes! She's away! She's loose in the room – now we'll never catch her.' He grabbed Stuart up and placed him on a table where he wouldn't be hit by a runaway car.

'Oh, mercy! Oh, mercy!' Stuart cried when he realized what he had done. It was a very awkward situation. Neither Dr Carey nor Stuart could see the little automobile, yet it was rushing all over the room under its own power, bumping into things. First there came a crashing noise over by the fireplace. The hearth broom fell down. Dr Carey leapt for the spot and pounced on the place where the sound had come from. But though he was quick, he had hardly got his hands on the place when there was another crash over by the wastebasket. The Doctor pounced again. Pounce! Crash! Pounce! Crash! The Doctor

was racing all over the room, pouncing and missing. It is almost impossible to catch a speedy invisible model automobile even when one is a skilful dentist.

'Oh, oh,' yelled Stuart, jumping up and down. 'I'm sorry, Dr Carey, I'm dreadfully sorry!'

'Get a butterfly net!' shouted the Doctor.

'I can't,' said Stuart. 'I'm not big enough to carry a butterfly net.'

'That's true,' said Dr Carey. 'I forgot. My apologies, Stuart.'

'The car is bound to stop sometime,' said Stuart, 'because it will run out of gas.'

'That's true, too,' said the Doctor. And so he and Stuart sat down and waited patiently until they no longer heard any crashing sounds in the room. Then the Doctor got down on his hands and knees and crawled cautiously all over, feeling here and there, until at last he found the car. It was in the fireplace, buried up to its hubs in wood ashes. The Doctor pressed the proper button and there it stood in plain sight again, its front fenders crumpled, its radiator leaking, its headlights broken, its windshield shattered, its right rear tire punctured, and quite a bit of yellow paint scratched off the hood.

'What a mess!' groaned the Doctor. 'Stuart, I hope this will be a lesson to you: never push a button on an automobile unless you are sure of what you are doing.'

'Yes, sir,' answered Stuart, and his eyes filled with tears, each tear being smaller than a drop of dew. It had been an unhappy morning, and Stuart was already homesick. He was sure that he was never going to see Margalo again.

12. The Schoolroom

WHILE Dr Carey was making repairs on the car, Stuart went shopping. He decided that, since he was about to take a long motor trip, he should have the proper clothes. He went to a doll's shop, where they had things which were the right size for him, and outfitted himself completely, with new luggage, suits, shirts, and accessories.

He charged everything and was well pleased with his purchases. That night he slept at the Doctor's apartment.

The next morning, Stuart started early, to avoid traffic. He thought it would be a good idea to get out on the road before there were too many cars and trucks. He drove through Central Park to One Hundred and Tenth Street, then over to the West Side Highway, then north to the Saw Mill River Parkway. The car ran beautifully and although people were inclined to stare at him, Stuart didn't mind. He was very careful not to press the button which had caused so much trouble the day before. He made up his mind that he would never use that button again.

Just as the sun was coming up, Stuart saw a man seated in thought by the side of the road. Stuart steered his car alongside, stopped, and put his head out.

'You're worried about something, aren't you?' asked Stuart.

'Yes, I am,' said the man, who was tall and mild.

'Can I help you in any way?' asked Stuart in a friendly voice.

The man shook his head. 'It's an impossible situation, I guess,' he replied. 'You see, I'm the Superintendent of Schools in this town.'

'That's not an impossible situation,' said Stuart. 'It's bad, but it's not impossible.'

'Well,' continued the man, 'I've always got problems that I can't solve. Today, for instance, one of my teachers is sick – Miss Gunderson her name is. She teaches Number Seven school.

I've got to find a substitute for her, a teacher who will take her place.'

'What's the matter with her?' asked Stuart.

'I don't know, exactly. The doctor says she may have rhinestones,' replied the Superintendent.

'Can't you find another teacher?' asked Stuart.

'No, that's the trouble. There's nobody in this town who knows anything; no spare teachers, no anything. School is supposed to begin in an hour.'

'I will be glad to take Miss Gunderson's place for a day, if you would like,' suggested Stuart agreeably.

The Superintendent of Schools looked up.

'Really?'

'Certainly,' said Stuart. 'Glad to.' He opened the door of the little car and stepped out. Walking around to the rear, he opened the baggage compartment and took out his

suitcase. 'If I'm to conduct a class in a schoolroom, I'd better take off these motoring togs and get into something more suitable,' he said. Stuart climbed the bank, went into the bushes, and was back in a few minutes wearing a pepper-and-salt jacket, old striped trousers, a Windsor tie, and spectacles. He folded his other clothes and packed them away in the suitcase.

'Do you think you can maintain discipline?' asked the Superintendent.

'Of course I can,' replied Stuart. 'I'll make the work interesting and the discipline will take care of itself. Don't worry about me.'

The man thanked him and they shook hands.

At quarter before nine the scholars had gathered in School Number Seven. When they missed Miss Gunderson and word got round that there would be a substitute, they were delighted.

'A substitute!' somebody whispered to somebody else. 'A substitute, a substitute!'

The news travelled fast, and soon everyone in the schoolroom knew that they were all to have a rest from Miss Gunderson for at least a day and were going to have the wonderful experience of being taught by a strange teacher whom nobody had ever seen before.

Stuart arrived at nine. He parked his car briskly at the door of the school, stalked boldly into the room, found a yardstick leaning against Miss Gunderson's desk, and climbed hand-over-hand to the top. There he found an inkwell, a pointer, some pens and pencils, a bottle of ink, some chalk, a bell, two hairpins, and three or four books in a pile. Stuart scrambled nimbly up to the top of the stack of books and jumped for the button on the bell. His weight was enough to make it ring, and Stuart promptly slid down, walked to the front of the desk, and said:

'Let me have your attention, please!'

The boys and girls crowded around the desk to look at the substitute. Everyone talked at once, and they seemed to be very much pleased. The girls giggled and the boys laughed and everyone's eyes lit up with excitement to see such a small and good-looking teacher, so appropriately dressed.

'Let me have your attention, please!' repeated Stuart. 'As you know, Miss Gunderson is sick and I am taking her place.'

'What's the matter with her?' asked Roy Hart, eagerly.

'Vitamin trouble,' replied Stuart. 'She took Vitamin D when she needed A. She took B when she was short of C, and her system became overloaded with riboflavin, thiamine hydrochloride, and even with pyridoxine, the need for which in human nutrition has not been established. Let it be a lesson for all of us!' He glared fiercely at the children and they made no more enquiries about Miss Gunderson.

'Everyone will now take his or her seat!' commanded Stuart. The pupils filed obediently down the aisles and dropped into their seats, and in a moment there was silence in the classroom. Stuart cleared his throat. Seizing a coat lapel in either hand, to make himself look like a professor, Stuart began:

'Anybody absent?'

The scholars shook their heads.

'Anybody late?'

They shook their heads.

'Very well,' said Stuart, 'what's the first subject you usually take up in the morning?'

'Arithmetic,' shouted the children.

'Bother arithmetic!' snapped Stuart. 'Let's skip it.'

There were wild shouts of enthusiasm at this suggestion. Everyone in the class seemed perfectly willing to skip arithmetic for one morning.

'What next do you study?' asked Stuart.

'Spelling,' cried the children.

'Well,' said Stuart, 'a misspelled word is an abomination in the sight of everyone. I consider it a very fine thing to spell words correctly and I strongly urge every one of you to buy a Webster's Collegiate Dictionary and consult it whenever you are in the slightest doubt. So much for spelling. What's next?'

The scholars were just as pleased to be let out of spelling as they were about arithmetic, and they shouted for joy, and everybody looked at everybody else and laughed and waved handkerchiefs and rulers, and some of the boys threw spit balls at some of the girls. Stuart had to climb on to the pile of books again and dive for the bell to restore order. 'What's next?' he repeated.

'Writing,' cried the scholars.

'Goodness,' said Stuart in disgust, 'don't you children know how to write yet?'

'Certainly we do!' yelled one and all.

'So much for that, then,' said Stuart.

'Social studies come next,' cried Elizabeth Gardner, eagerly.

'Social studies? Never heard of them,' said Stuart. 'Instead of taking up any special subject this morning, why wouldn't it be a good idea if we just talked about something.'

The scholars glanced around at each other in expectancy.

'Could we talk about the way it feels to hold a snake in your hand and then it winds itself around your wrist?' asked Arthur Greenlaw.

'We could, but I'd rather not,' replied Stuart.

'Could we talk about sin and vice?' pleaded Lydia Lacey.

'Nope,' said Stuart. 'Try again.'

'Could we talk about the fat woman at the circus and she had hair all over her chin?' begged Isidor Feinberg, reminiscently.

'No,' said Stuart. 'I'll tell you, let's talk about the King of the World.' He looked all around the room hopefully to see how the children liked that idea.

'There isn't any King of the World,' said Harry Jamieson in disgust.

'What's the diff?' said Stuart. 'There *ought* to be one.'

'Kings are old-fashioned,' said Harry.

'Well, all right then, let's talk about the Chairman of the World. The world gets into a lot of trouble because it has no chairman. I would like to be Chairman of the World myself.'

'You're too small,' said Mary Bendix.

'Oh, fish feathers!' said Stuart. 'Size has nothing to do with it. It's temperament and ability that count. The Chairman has to have ability and he must know what's important. How many of you know what's important?'

Up went all the hands.

'Very good,' said Stuart, cocking one leg across the other and shoving his hands in the pockets of his jacket. 'Henry Rackmeyer, you tell us what is important.'

'A shaft of sunlight at the end of a dark afternoon, a note in music, and the way the back of a baby's neck smells if its mother keeps it tidy,' answered Henry.

'Correct,' said Stuart. 'Those are the important things. You forgot one thing, though. Mary Bendix, what did Henry Rackmeyer forget?'

'He forgot ice cream with chocolate sauce on it,' said Mary quickly.

'Exactly,' said Stuart. 'Ice cream is important. Well now, if I'm going to be Chairman of the World this morning, we've got to have some rules, otherwise it will be too confusing, with everyone running every which way and helping himself to things and nobody behaving. We've got to have some laws if we're going to play this game. Can anybody suggest any good laws for the world?'

Albert Fernstrom raised his hand. 'Don't eat mushrooms, they might be toadstools,' suggested Albert.

'That's not a law,' said Stuart, 'that's merely a bit of friendly advice. Very good advice, Albert, but advice and law are not the same. Law is much more solemn than advice. Law is extremely solemn. Anybody else think of a law for the world?'

'Nix on swiping anything,' suggested John Poldowski, solemnly.

'Very good,' said Stuart. 'Good law.'

'Never poison anything but rats,' said Anthony Brendisi.

'That's no good,' said Stuart. 'It's unfair to rats. A law has to be fair to everybody.'

Anthony looked sulky. 'But rats are unfair to us,' he said. 'Rats are objectionable.'

'I know they are,' said Stuart. 'But from a

rat's point of view, poison is objectionable. A Chairman has to see all sides to a problem.'

'Have you got a rat's point of view?' asked Anthony. 'You look a little like a rat.'

'No,' replied Stuart, 'I have more the point of view of a mouse, which is very different. I see things whole. It's obvious to me that rats are underprivileged. They've never been able to get out in the open.'

'Rats don't like the open,' said Agnes Beretska.

'That's because whenever they come out, somebody socks them. Rats might like the open if they were allowed to use it. Any other ideas for laws?'

Agnes Beretska raised her hand. 'There ought to be a law against fighting.'

'Impractical,' said Stuart. 'Men like to fight. But you're getting warm, Agnes.'

'No scrapping?' asked Agnes, timidly. Stuart shook his head.

'Absolutely no being mean,' suggested Mildred Hoffenstein.

'Very fine law,' said Stuart. 'When I am Chairman, anybody who is mean to anybody else is going to catch it.'

'That won't work,' remarked Herbert Prendergast. 'Some people are just naturally mean. Albert Fernstrom is always being mean to me.'

'I'm not saying it'll work,' said Stuart. 'It's a good law and we'll give it a try. We'll give it a try right here and now. Somebody do something mean to somebody. Harry Jamieson, you be mean to Katharine Stableford. Wait a minute, now, what's that you've got in your hand, Katharine?'

'It's a little tiny pillow stuffed with sweet balsam.'

'Does it say "For you I pine, for you I balsam" on it?'

'Yes,' said Katharine.

'Do you love it very much?' asked Stuart.

'Yes, I do,' said Katharine.

'OK, Harry, grab it, take it away!'

Harry ran over to where Katharine sat, grabbed the little pillow from her hand, and ran back to his seat, while Katharine screamed.

'Now then,' said Stuart in a fierce voice, 'hold on, my good people, while your Chairman consults the book of rules!' He pretended to thumb through a book. 'Here we are. Page 492. "Absolutely no being mean." Page 560. "Nix on swiping anything." Harry Jamieson has broken two laws – the law against being mean and the law against swiping. Let's get Harry and set him back before he becomes so mean people will hardly recognize him any more! Come on!'

Stuart ran for the yardstick and slid down, like a fireman coming down a pole in a firehouse. He ran toward Harry, and the other children jumped up from their seats and raced up and down the aisles and crowded around Harry while Stuart demanded that he give up the little pillow. Harry looked frightened, although he knew it was just a test. He gave Katharine the pillow.

'There, it worked pretty well,' said Stuart. 'No being mean is a perfectly good law.' He wiped his face with his handkerchief, for he was quite warm from the exertion of being Chairman of the World. It had taken more running and leaping and sliding than he had imagined. Katharine was very much pleased to have her pillow back.

'Let's see that little pillow a minute,' said Stuart, whose curiosity was beginning to get the better of him. Katharine showed it to him. It was about as long as Stuart was high, and Stuart suddenly thought what a fine sweet-smelling bed it would make for him. He began to want the pillow himself.

'That's a very pretty thing,' said Stuart, trying to hide his eagerness. 'You don't want to sell it, do you?'

'Oh, no,' replied Katharine. 'It was a present to me.'

'I suppose it was given you by a boy you met at Lake Hopatcong last summer, and it reminds you of him,' murmured Stuart, dreamily.

'Yes, it was,' said Katharine, blushing.

'Ah,' said Stuart, 'summers are wonderful, aren't they, Katharine?'

'Yes, and last summer was the most wonderful summer I have ever had in all my life.'

'I can imagine,' replied Stuart. 'You're sure you wouldn't want to sell that little pillow?'

Katharine shook her head.

'Don't know as I blame you,' replied Stuart, quietly. 'Summertime is important. It's like a shaft of sunlight.'

'Or a note in music,' said Elizabeth Acheson.

'Or the way the back of a baby's neck smells if its mother keeps it tidy,' said Marilyn Roberts.

Stuart sighed. 'Never forget your summertimes, my dears,' he said. 'Well, I've got to be getting along. It's been a pleasure to know you all. Class is dismissed!'

Stuart strode rapidly to the door, climbed into the car, and with a final wave of the hand drove off in a northerly direction, while the children raced alongside and screamed 'Goodbye, goodbye, goodbye!' They all wished they could have a substitute every day, instead of Miss Gunderson.

13. Ames' Crossing

IN THE loveliest town of all, where the houses were white and high and the elm trees were green and higher than the houses, where the front yards were wide and pleasant and the back yards were bushy and worth finding out about, where the streets sloped down to the stream and the stream flowed quietly under the bridge, where the lawns ended in orchards and the orchards ended in fields and the fields ended in pastures and the pastures climbed the hill and disappeared over the top toward the wonderful wide sky,

in this loveliest of all towns Stuart stopped to
get a drink of sarsaparilla.

Parking his car in front of the general store,
he stepped out and the sun felt so good that
he sat down on the porch for a few moments
to enjoy the feeling of being in a new place on
a fine day. This was the most peaceful and
beautiful spot he had found in all his travels.
It seemed to him a place he would gladly
spend the rest of his life in, if it weren't that he

might get homesick for the sights of New York and for his family, Mr and Mrs Frederick C. Little and George, and if it weren't for the fact that something deep inside him made him want to find Margalo.

After a while the storekeeper came out to smoke a cigarette, and he joined Stuart on the front steps. He started to offer Stuart a cigarette but when he noticed how small he was, he changed his mind.

'Have you any sarsaparilla in your store?' asked Stuart. 'I've got a ruinous thirst.'

'Certainly,' said the storekeeper. 'Gallons of it. Sarsaparilla, root beer, birch beer, ginger ale, Moxie, lemon soda, Coca Cola, Pepsi Cola, Dipsi Cola, Pipsi Cola, Popsi Cola, and raspberry cream tonic. Anything you want.'

'Let me have a bottle of sarsaparilla, please,' said Stuart, 'and a paper cup.'

The storekeeper went back into the store and returned with the drink. He opened the bottle, poured some out into the cup, and set

the cup down on the step below Stuart, who
whipped off his cap, lay down on his stomach,
and dipped up some of the cool refreshing
drink, using his cap as a dipper.

'That's very refreshing,' remarked Stuart.
'There's nothing like a long, cool drink in the
heat of the day, when you're travelling.'

'Are you going far?' asked the storekeeper.

'Perhaps *very* far,' replied Stuart. 'I'm
looking for a bird named Margalo. You
haven't sighted her, have you?'

'Can't say I have,' said the storekeeper.
'What does she look like?'

'Perfectly beautiful,' replied Stuart, wiping
the sarsaparilla off his lips with the corner of
his sleeve. 'She's a remarkable bird. Anybody

would notice her. She comes from a place where there are thistles.'

The storekeeper looked at Stuart closely.

'How tall are you?' he asked.

'You mean in my stocking feet?' said Stuart.

'Yes.'

'Two inches nothing and a quarter,' answered Stuart. 'I haven't been measured recently, however. I may have shot up a bit.'

'You know,' said the storekeeper, thoughtfully, 'there's somebody in this town you really ought to meet.'

'Who's that?' asked Stuart, yawning.

'Harriet Ames,' said the storekeeper. 'She's just your size – maybe a trifle shorter, if anything.'

'What's she like?' asked Stuart. 'Fair, fat, and forty?'

'No, Harriet is young and she is quite pretty. She is considered one of the best dressed girls in this town, too. All her clothes are tailored specially for her.'

'That so?' remarked Stuart.

'Yes. Harriet's quite a girl. Her people, the Ameses, are rather prominent in this town. One of her ancestors used to be the ferryman here in Revolutionary days. He would carry anybody across the stream – he didn't care whether they were British soldiers or American soldiers, as long as they paid their fare. I guess he did pretty well. Anyway, the Ameses have always had plenty of money. They live in a big house with a lot of servants. I know Harriet would be very much interested to meet you.'

'That's very kind of you,' replied Stuart, 'but I'm not much of a society man these days. Too much on the move. I never stay long anywhere – I blow into a town and blow right out again, here today, gone tomorrow, a will o' the wisp. The highways and byways are where you'll find me, always looking for Margalo. Sometimes I feel that I'm quite near to her and that she's just around the turn of the road. Other times I feel that I'll never find her and never hear her voice again. Which reminds me, it's time I was on my way.' Stuart paid for his drink, said goodbye to the storekeeper, and drove off.

But Ames' Crossing seemed like the finest town he had ever known, and before he reached the end of the main street he swerved sharp left, turned off on to a dirt road, and drove down to a quiet spot on the bank of the river. That afternoon he swam and lay on his back on the mossy bank, his hands crossed under his head, his thoughts returning to the conversation he had had with the storekeeper.

'Harriet Ames,' he murmured.

Evening came, and Stuart still lingered by the stream. He ate a light supper of a cheese sandwich and a drink of water, and slept that night in the warm grass with the sound of the stream in his ears.

In the morning the sun rose warm and bright and Stuart slipped into the river again for an early dip. After breakfast he left his car hidden under a skunk cabbage leaf and walked up to the post office. While he was filling his fountain pen from the public inkwell he happened to glance toward the door and what

he saw startled him so that he almost lost his balance and fell into the ink. A girl about two inches high had entered and was crossing the floor toward the mail boxes. She wore sports clothes and walked with her head held high. In her hair was a stamen from a flower.

Stuart began to tremble from excitement.

'Must be the Ames girl,' he said to himself. And he kept out of sight behind the inkwell as he watched her open her mail box, which was about a quarter of an inch wide, and pull out her letters. The storekeeper had told the truth:

Harriet was pretty. And of course she was the only girl Stuart had ever encountered who wasn't miles and miles taller than he was. Stuart figured that if the two of them were to walk along together, her head would come a little higher than his shoulder. The idea filled him with interest. He wanted to slide down to the floor and speak to her, but he didn't dare. All his boldness had left him and he stayed hidden behind the inkwell until Harriet had gone. When he was sure that she was out of sight, he stole out of the post office and slunk down the street to the store, half hoping that he would meet the beautiful little girl, half fearing that he would.

'Have you any engraved stationery?' he asked the storekeeper. 'I'm behind on my correspondence.'

The storekeeper helped Stuart up on to the counter and found some letter paper for him – small paper, marked with the initial 'L.' Stuart whipped out his fountain pen and sat down

against a five-cent candy bar and began a
letter to Harriet:

'MY DEAR MISS AMES,' he wrote. 'I am a
young person of modest proportions. By birth
I am a New Yorker, but at the moment I am
travelling on business of a confidential nature.
My travels have brought me to your village.
Yesterday the keeper of your local
store, who has an honest face
and an open manner, gave
me a most favourable
report of your character
and appearance.'

At this point in the
letter Stuart's pen ran
dry from the long words

and Stuart had to get the storekeeper to lower him head-first into a bottle of ink so that he could refill the pen. Then he went back to letter writing . . .

'Pray forgive me, Miss Ames,' continued Stuart, 'for presuming to strike up an acquaintance on so slender an excuse as your physical similarity; but of course the fact is, as you yourself must know, there are very few people who are only two inches in height. I say "two inches" – actually I am somewhat taller than that. My only drawback is that I look something like a mouse. I am nicely proportioned, however. Am also muscular beyond my years. Let me be perfectly blunt: my purpose in writing this brief note is to suggest that we meet. I realize that your parents may object to the suddenness and directness of my proposal, as well as to my somewhat mouselike appearance, so I think probably it might be a good idea if you just didn't mention the matter to them. What they don't know won't hurt them. However, you probably understand more about dealing with your father and mother than I do, so I won't attempt to instruct you but will leave everything to your good judgement.

'Being an outdoors person, I am camped by the river in an attractive spot at the foot of Tracy's Lane. Would you care to go for a paddle with me in my canoe? How about tomorrow afternoon toward sundown, when the petty annoyances of the day are behind us and the river seems to flow more quietly in the long shadows of the willows? These tranquil spring evenings are designed by special architects for the enjoyment of boatmen. I love the water, dear Miss Ames, and my canoe is like an old and trusted friend.'

Stuart forgot, in the excitement of writing Harriet, that he did not own a canoe.

'If you wish to accept my invitation, be at the river tomorrow about five o'clock. I shall await your arrival with all the eagerness I can muster. And now I must close this offensive letter and catch up with my affairs.

Yours very truly,
STUART LITTLE.'

After Stuart had sealed his letter in an envelope, he turned to the storekeeper.

'Where can I get hold of a canoe?' he asked.

'Right here,' replied the storekeeper. He walked over to his souvenir counter and took down a little birchbark canoe with the words SUMMER MEMORIES stamped on the side. Stuart examined it closely.

'Does she leak?' asked Stuart.

'It's a nice canoe,' replied the storekeeper, bending it gently back into shape with his fingers. 'It will cost you seventy-five cents plus a penny tax.'

Stuart took out his money and paid the man. Then he looked inside the canoe and noticed that there were no paddles.

'What about paddles?' he said, making his voice sound businesslike. The storekeeper hunted around among the souvenirs but he couldn't seem to find any paddles, so he went over to the ice cream counter and came back with two little cardboard spoons – the kind you use for eating ice cream on picnics.

'These will work out all right as paddles,' he said.

Stuart took the spoons, but he was disgusted with the looks of them.

'They may work out all right,' said Stuart, 'but I would hate to meet an American Indian while I had one of *these* things in my hand.'

The storekeeper carried the canoe and the paddles out in front of the store and set them down in the street. He wondered what this tiny boatman would do next, but Stuart never hesitated. Taking a piece of thread from his pocket, he lashed the paddles to the thwarts, swung the canoe lightly up on his head, and walked off with it as calmly as though he were a Canadian guide. He was very proud of his ability with boats and he liked to show off.

14. An Evening on the River

WHEN Stuart arrived at his camp site by the river, he was tired and hot. He put the canoe in the water and was sorry to see that it leaked badly. The birch bark at the stern was held together by a lacing, and the water came in through the seam. In a very few seconds the canoe was half full of water.

'Darn it!' said Stuart, 'I've been swindled.' He had paid seventy-six cents for a genuine Indian birchbark canoe, only to find that it leaked.

'Darn, darn, darn,' he muttered.

Then he bailed out his canoe and hauled it up on the beach for repairs. He knew he couldn't take Harriet out in a leaky boat – she wouldn't like it. Tired though he was, he climbed a spruce tree and found some spruce gum. With this he plugged the seam and stopped the leak. Even so, the canoe turned out to be a cranky little craft. If Stuart had not had plenty of experience on the water, he would have got into serious trouble with it. It was a tippy boat even for a souvenir. Stuart carried stones from the beach down to the water's edge and ballasted the canoe with the stones until it floated evenly and

steadily. He made a backrest so that Harriet would be able to lean back and trail her fingers in the water if she wished. He also made a pillow by tying one of his clean handkerchiefs around some moss. Then he went for a paddle to practise his stroke. He was angry that he didn't have anything better than a paper spoon for a paddle, but he decided that there was nothing he could do about it. He wondered whether Harriet would notice that his paddle was really just an ice cream spoon.

All that afternoon Stuart worked on the canoe, adjusting ballast, filling seams, and getting everything shipshape for the morrow. He could think of nothing else but his date with Harriet. At suppertime he took his axe, felled a dandelion,

opened a can of deviled ham,

and had a light supper of ham and dandelion milk. After supper, he propped himself up against a fern, bit off some spruce gum for a chew, and lay there on the bank dreaming and chewing gum. In his imagination he went over every detail of tomorrow's trip with Harriet. With his eyes shut he seemed to see the whole occasion plainly – how she would look when she came down the path to the water, how calm and peaceful the river was going to be in the twilight, how graceful the canoe would seem, drawn up on the shore. In imagination he lived every minute of their evening together. They would paddle to a large water-lily pad upstream, and he would invite Harriet to step out on the pad and sit awhile. Stuart planned to wear his swimming trunks under his clothes so that he could dive off the lily pad into the cool stream. He would swim the crawl stroke,

up and down and all around the lily pad,
while Harriet watched, admiring his ability as
a swimmer. (Stuart chewed the spruce gum
very rapidly as he thought about this part of
the episode.)

Suddenly Stuart opened his eyes and sat up.
He thought about the letter he had sent and
he wondered whether it had ever been
delivered. It was an unusually small letter, of
course, and might have gone unnoticed in the
letterbox. This idea filled him with fears and
worries. But soon he let his thoughts return to

the river, and as he lay there a whippoorwill began to sing on the opposite shore, darkness spread over the land, and Stuart dropped off to sleep.

The next day dawned cloudy. Stuart had to go up to the village to have the oil changed in his car, so he hid the canoe under some leaves, tied it firmly to a stone, and went off on his errand, still thinking about Harriet and wishing it were a nicer day. The sky looked rainy.

Stuart returned from the village with a headache, but he hoped that it would be better before five o'clock. He felt rather nervous, as he had never taken a girl canoeing before. He spent the afternoon lying around camp, trying on different shirts to see which looked best on him and combing his whiskers. He would no sooner get a clean shirt on than he would discover that it was wet under the arms, from nervous perspiration, and he would have to change it for a dry one. He put on a clean shirt at two o'clock, another at three o'clock, and another at quarter past four. This took up most of the afternoon. As five o'clock drew near, Stuart grew more and more nervous. He kept looking at his watch, glancing up the path, combing his hair, talking to himself, and fidgeting. The day had turned chilly and Stuart was almost sure that there was going to be rain. He couldn't imagine what he would do if it should rain just as Harriet Ames showed up to go canoeing.

At last five o'clock arrived. Stuart heard someone coming down the path. It was Harriet. She had accepted his invitation. Stuart threw himself down against a stump and tried to strike an easy attitude, as though he were accustomed to taking girls out. He waited till Harriet was within a few feet of him, then got up.

'Hello there,' he said, trying to keep his voice from trembling.

'Are you Mr Little?' asked Harriet.

'Yes,' said Stuart. 'It's nice of you to come.'

'Well, it was very good of you to ask me,' replied Harriet. She was wearing a white sweater, a tweed skirt, short white wool socks, and sneakers. Her hair was tied with a bright coloured handkerchief, and Stuart noticed that she carried a box of peppermints in her hand.

'Not at all, glad to do it,' said Stuart. 'I only wish we had better weather. Looks rather sticky, don't you think?' Stuart was trying to make his voice sound as though he had an English accent.

Harriet looked at the sky and nodded. 'Oh, well,' she said, 'if it rains, it rains.'

'Sure,' repeated Stuart, 'if it rains, it rains. My canoe is a short distance up the shore. May I help you over the rough places in the path?' Stuart was a courteous mouse by nature, but Harriet said she didn't need any help. She was an active girl and not at all inclined to stumble or fall. Stuart led the way to where he had hidden the canoe, and Harriet followed, but when they reached the spot Stuart was horrified to discover that the canoe was not there. It had disappeared.

Stuart's heart sank. He felt like crying.

'The canoe is gone,' he groaned.

Then he began racing wildly up and down the bank, looking everywhere. Harriet joined in the search, and after a while they found the canoe – but it was a mess. Someone had been playing with it. A long piece of heavy string was tied to one end. The ballast rocks were gone. The pillow was gone. The backrest was gone. The spruce gum had come out of the seam. Mud was all over everything, and one of the paddles was all bent and twisted. It was just a mess. It looked just the way a birchbark canoe looks after some big boys are finished playing with it.

Stuart was heartbroken. He did not know
what to do. He sat down on a twig and buried
his head in his hands. 'Oh, gee,' he kept saying,
'oh, gee whiz.'

'What's the trouble?' asked Harriet.

'Miss Ames,' said Stuart in a trembling
voice, 'I assure you I had everything beautifully
arranged – *everything*. And now look!'

Harriet was for fixing the canoe up and
going out on the river anyway, but Stuart
couldn't stand that idea.

'It's no use,' he said bitterly, 'it wouldn't be
the same.'

'The same as what?' asked Harriet.

'The same as the way it was going to be,
when I was thinking about it yesterday. I'm
afraid a woman can't understand these things.

Look at that string! It's tied on so tight I could never get it off.'

'Well,' suggested Harriet, 'couldn't we just let it hang over in the water and trail along after us?'

Stuart looked at her in despair. 'Did you ever see an Indian paddling along some quiet unspoiled river with a great big piece of rope dragging astern?' he asked.

'We could pretend we were fishing,' said Harriet, who didn't realize that some people are fussy about boats.

'I don't *want* to pretend I'm fishing,' cried Stuart, desperately. 'Besides, look at that mud! *Look* at it!' He was screaming now.

Harriet sat down on the twig beside Stuart. She offered him a peppermint but he shook his head.

'Well,' she said, 'it's starting to rain, and I guess I'd better be running along if you are not going to take me paddling in your canoe. I don't see why you have to sit here and sulk.

Would you like to come up to my house? After dinner you could take me to the dance at the Country Club. It might cheer you up.'

'No, thank you,' replied Stuart. 'I don't know how to dance. Besides, I plan to make an early start in the morning. I'll probably be on the road at daybreak.'

'Are you going to sleep out in all this rain?' asked Harriet.

'Certainly,' said Stuart. 'I'll crawl in under the canoe.'

Harriet shrugged her shoulders. 'Well,' she said, 'goodbye, Mr Little.'

'Goodbye, Miss Ames,' said Stuart. 'I am sorry our evening on the river had to end like this.'

'So am I,' said Harriet. And she walked away along the wet path towards Tracy's Lane, leaving Stuart alone with his broken dreams and his damaged canoe.

15. Heading North

STUART slept under the canoe that night.
He awakened at four to find that the rain
had stopped. The day would break clear.
Already the birds were beginning to stir and
make bright sounds in the branches overhead.
Stuart never let a bird pass without looking to
see if it was Margalo.

At the edge of the town he found a filling
station and stopped to take on some gas.

'Five, please,' said Stuart to the attendant.

The man looked at the tiny automobile in
amazement.

'Five what?' he asked.

'Five drops,' said Stuart. But the man shook his head and said that he couldn't sell such a small amount of gas.

'Why can't you?' demanded Stuart. 'You need the money and I need the gas. Why can't we work something out between us?'

The filling station man went inside and came back with a medicine dropper. Stuart unscrewed the cap of the tank and the man put in five drops of gasoline. 'I've never done anything like this before,' he said.

'Better look at the oil, too,' said Stuart.

After everything had been checked and the money had been paid, Stuart climbed in, started the engine, and drove out on to the highway. The sky was growing brighter, and along the river the mists of morning hung in the early light. The village was still asleep. Stuart's car purred along smoothly. Stuart felt refreshed and glad to be on the move again.

Half a mile out of town the road forked. One road seemed to go off toward the west, the other road continued north. Stuart drew up to the side of the northbound road and got out to look the situation over. To his surprise he discovered that there was a man sitting in the ditch, leaning against a signpost. The man wore spurs on his legs. He also wore a heavy leather belt, and Stuart realized that he must be a repairman for the telephone company.

'Good morning,' said Stuart in a friendly voice. The repairman raised one hand to his head in a salute. Stuart sat down in the ditch beside him and breathed deeply of the fresh,

sweet air. 'It's going to be a fine day,' he observed.

'Yes,' agreed the repairman, 'a fine day. I am looking forward to climbing my poles.'

'I wish you fair skies and a tight grip,' said Stuart. 'By the way, do you ever see any birds at the tops of your poles?'

'Yes, I see birds in great numbers,' replied the repairman.

'Well, if you ever run across a bird named Margalo,' said Stuart, 'I'd appreciate it if you would drop me a line. Here's my card.'

'Describe the bird,' said the repairman, taking out pad and pencil.

'Brown,' said Stuart. 'Brown, with a streak of yellow on her bosom.'

'Know where she comes from?' asked the man.

'She comes from fields once tall with wheat, from pastures deep in fern and thistle; she comes from vales of meadowsweet, and she loves to whistle.'

The repairman wrote it all down briefly. 'Fields – wheat – pastures, fern & thistle. Vales, meadowsweet. Enjoys whistling.' Then he put the pad back in his pocket, and tucked Stuart's card away in his wallet. 'I'll keep my eyes open,' he promised.

Stuart thanked him. They sat for a while in silence. Then the man spoke.

'Which direction are you headed?' he asked.

'North,' said Stuart.

'North is nice,' said the repairman. 'I've always enjoyed going north. Of course, south-west is a fine direction, too.'

'Yes, I suppose it is,' said Stuart, thoughtfully.

'And there's east,' continued the repairman. 'I once had an interesting experience on an easterly course. Do you want me to tell you about it?'

'No, thanks,' said Stuart.

The repairman seemed disappointed, but he kept right on talking. 'There's something about north,' he said, 'something that sets it apart from all other directions. A person who is heading north is not making any mistake, in my opinion.'

'That's the way I look at it,' said Stuart. 'I rather expect that from now on I shall be travelling north until the end of my days.'

'Worse things than that could happen to a person,' said the repairman.

'Yes, I know,' answered Stuart.

'Following a broken telephone line north, I have come upon some wonderful places,' continued the repairman. 'Swamps where cedars grow and turtles wait on logs but not for anything in particular; fields bordered by

crooked fences broken by years of standing still; orchards so old they have forgotten where the farmhouse is. In the north I have eaten my lunch in pastures rank with ferns and junipers, all under fair skies with a wind blowing. My business has taken me into spruce woods on winter nights where the snow lay deep and soft, a perfect place for a carnival of rabbits. I have sat at peace on the freight platforms of railroad junctions in the north, in the warm hours and with the warm smells. I know fresh lakes in the north, undisturbed except by fish and hawk and, of course, by the Telephone Company, which has to follow its nose. I know all these places well. They are a long way from here – don't forget that. And a person who is looking for something doesn't travel very fast.'

'That's perfectly true,' said Stuart. 'Well, I guess I'd better be going. Thank you for your friendly remarks.'

'Not at all,' said the repairman. 'I hope you find that bird.'

Stuart rose from the ditch, climbed into his car, and started up the road that led toward the north. The sun was just coming up over the hills on his right. As he peered ahead into the great land that stretched before him, the way seemed long. But the sky was bright, and he somehow felt he was headed in the right direction.

E.B. WHITE

Stuart
Little

ABOUT THE AUTHOR

E. B. WHITE

1899	Born 11 July in Mount Vernon, New York, USA
1921	Graduated from Cornell University
1922	Became a reporter for the Seattle Times newspaper
1927	Appointed a contributing editor to the New Yorker magazine, where he met his wife, Katharine
1945	Stuart Little published
1952	Charlotte's Web published
1959	Co-authored The Elements of Style (a book for writers)
1970	The Trumpet of the Swan published
1971	Awarded the National Medal for Literature
1985	Died at home in Maine, USA, on 1 October

INTERESTING FACTS

E. B. White was the youngest of six children. His father was a piano manufacturer. He never liked his name, Elwyn, and used his college nickname, 'Andy', for the rest of his life.

DID YOU LIKE THE PICTURES
IN *STUART LITTLE*?

Garth Williams's illustrations haven't changed since the very first edition of Stuart Little *was published in 1945. He also illustrated* Charlotte's Web *by E. B. White, the* Little House on the Prairie *series by Laura Ingalls Wilder and many other children's classics.*

Look closely at the drawings and you'll see that they're very detailed, with lots of lines and shading to create texture, action and emotion.

INTERESTING FACTS

As well as his work as an illustrator, Garth Williams was also a prize-winning sculptor.

WHERE DID THE
STORY COME FROM?

*It is said that Stuart Little first appeared to
E. B. White in a dream, while he was in a railway
sleeping car. Twenty years later, he wrote a few
short stories about a boy who looked like a mouse,
and that idea finally grew into an entire book – the
book which you have just finished reading!*

GUESS WHO?

A

He was only about **two inches high;** and he had a mouse's sharp nose, a mouse's tail, a mouse's whiskers, and the pleasant, shy manner of a mouse.

B

[He] was lying on the rug in the middle of the room, thinking about the days when he was just a **kitten.**

C

Soon she felt much better and went **hopping** around the house, examining everything with the greatest care and interest.

ANSWERS: A) *Stuart Little* B) *Snowbell* C) *Margalo*

WORDS GLORIOUS WORDS!

Lots of words have several different meanings – here are a few you'll find in this Puffin book. Use a **dictionary** or look them up online to find other definitions.

consternation

a feeling of anxiety or dismay, usually at something unexpected

bronchitis

an illness that makes you cough a lot

stationery

writing paper and other office materials

schooner

a sailing ship with two or more masts, typically with the foremast smaller than the mainmast

Windsor tie

a wide silk necktie secured loosely in a double knot

spyglass

a hand-held telescope

inch

an old-fashioned measure of length; an inch is approximately 2.5cm

DID YOU KNOW?

E. B. White *began* **Stuart Little** *in the hope of amusing his young niece, but before he had finished it she had grown up.*

E. B. White received several letters from people also called **Stuart Little** *– one such person claimed angrily that he was going to write a children's book about* **a rat** *named E. B. White!*

Stuart Little *was the* **first** *children's book that E. B. White had ever* **written***, and was also the first that Garth Williams had ever* **illustrated***.*

QUIZ

Thinking caps on – let's see how much you can remember! Answers are at the bottom of the opposite page. (No peeking!)

1 *What is the name of the boat that Stuart sails in the boat race?*

a) Wasp

b) Carbuncle

c) Songbird

d) Whistler

2 *How tall is Harriet Ames?*

a) *2 inches*

b) *6 inches*

c) *1 metre*

d) *27 centimetres*

3 **In which city does Stuart Little live?**

a) London

b) New York

c) Amsterdam

d) Gotham

4 **What is the name of Mrs Little's cat?**

a) Snowy

b) Snow White

c) Snowball

d) Snowbell

> **STUART
> LITTLE SAYS:**
> '. . . a misspelled word is an abomination in the sight of everyone.'

5 **What was Stuart's first job?**

a) Teacher

b) Dentist

c) Pilot

d) Vet

MAKE
AND
DO

How to ***draw a mouse***

1 Using a pencil, draw a large circle with a triangle for the head.

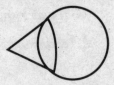

2 Draw circles for the ears, then add a smaller circle for the eye, and an even smaller one for the nose.

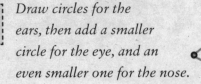

3 Add two circles overlapping each other for the body.

4 For the legs, draw two small ovals each (with a larger set for the back legs), and two smaller circles with little finger shapes for the paws.

5 Outline your mouse and add a long thin tail, whiskers and claws.

6 Rub out all of the inner pencil lines and colour your mouse with whichever colours you choose. You could even give your mouse a jumper, or a hat – just like Stuart Little!

IN THIS YEAR

1945
Fact Pack

What else was happening in the world when this Puffin book was published?

World War Two ends and, to celebrate, street parties are held across Great Britain.

The best-selling UK author **Jacqueline Wilson** is born.

The Friendly Ghost, the first **'noveltoon'** (an animated cartoon) featuring Casper is released.

PUFFIN
WRITING
TIP

Keep a travel journal when you go on holiday so that you can capture all the exciting new sights and sounds.

STUART LITTLE SAYS:

'I ran away from home this morning. I am going out into the world to seek my fortune and to look for a lost bird.'

If you have enjoyed *Stuart Little*, you may like to read *The Trumpet of the Swan* in which you'll meet Louis – the most extraordinay swan ever!

7. School Days

A FEW days after the swans arrived at their winter home on the Red Rock Lakes, Louis had an idea. He decided that since he was unable to use his voice, he should learn to read and write. 'If I'm defective in one respect,' he said to himself, 'I should try and develop myself along other lines. I will learn to read and write. Then I will hang a small slate around my neck and carry a chalk pencil. In that way I will be able to communicate with anybody who can read.'

Louis liked company, and he already had

many friends on the lakes. The place was a refuge for water birds – swans, geese, ducks, and other waterfowl. They lived there because it was a safe place and because the water stayed warm even in the coldest winter weather. Louis was greatly admired for his ability as a swimmer. He liked to compete with other cygnets to see who could swim under water the greatest distance and stay down the longest.

When Louis had fully made up his mind about learning to read and write, he decided to visit Sam Beaver and get help from him. 'Perhaps,' thought Louis, 'Sam will let me go to school with him, and the teacher will show me how to write.' The idea excited him. He wondered whether a young swan would be accepted in a classroom of children. He wondered whether it was hard to learn to read. Most of all, he wondered whether he could find Sam. Montana is a big state, and he wasn't even sure Sam lived in Montana, but he hoped he did.

Next morning, when his parents were not looking, Louis took off into the air. He flew northeast. When he came to the Yellowstone River, he followed it to the Sweet Grass country. When he saw a town beneath him, he landed next to the schoolhouse and waited for the boys and girls to be let out. Louis looked at every boy, hoping to see Sam. But Sam wasn't there.

'Wrong town, wrong school,' thought Louis. 'I'll try again.' He flew off, found another town, and located the school, but all the boys and girls had gone home for the day.

'I'll just have a look around anyway,' thought Louis. He didn't dare walk down the main street, for fear somebody would shoot him. Instead, he took to the air and circled around, flying low and looking carefully at every boy in sight. After about ten minutes, he saw a ranch house where a boy was splitting wood near the kitchen door. The boy had black hair. Louis glided down.

lucky,' he thought. 'It's Sam.'

When Sam saw the swan, he laid down his axe and stood perfectly still. Louis walked up timidly, then reached down and untied Sam's shoelace.

'Hello!' said Sam in a friendly voice.

Louis tried to say ko-hoh, but not a sound came from his throat.

'I know *you*,' said Sam. 'You're the one that never said anything and used to pull my shoelaces.'

Louis nodded.

'I'm glad to see you,' said Sam. 'What can I do for you?'

Louis just stared straight ahead.

'Are you hungry?' asked Sam.

Louis shook his head.

'Thirsty?'

Louis shook his head.

'Do you want to stay overnight with us, here at the ranch?' asked Sam.

Louis nodded his head and jumped up and down.

'OK,' said Sam. 'We have plenty of room. It's just a question of getting my father's permission.'

Sam picked up his axe, laid a stick of wood on the chopping block, and split the stick neatly down the middle. He looked at Louis.

'There's something wrong with your voice, isn't there?' he asked.

Louis nodded, pumping his neck up and down hard. He knew Sam was his friend, although he didn't know that Sam had once saved his mother's life.

In a few minutes Mr Beaver rode into the yard on a cow pony. He got off and tied his pony to a rail. 'What have you got there?' he asked Sam.

'It's a young Trumpeter Swan,' said Sam. 'He's only a few months old. Will you let me keep him awhile?'

'Well,' said Mr Beaver, 'I think it's against the law to hold one of these wild birds in captivity. But I'll phone the game warden and see what he says. If he says yes, you can keep him.'

'Tell the warden the swan has something the matter with him,' called Sam as his father started toward the house.

'What's wrong with him?' asked his father.

'He has a speech problem,' replied Sam. 'Something's wrong with his throat.'

'What are you talking about? Who ever heard of a swan with a speech problem?'

'Well,' said Sam, 'this is a Trumpeter Swan that can't trumpet. He's defective. He can't make a sound.'

Mr Beaver looked at his son as though he didn't know whether to believe him or not. But he went into the house. In a few minutes he came back. 'The warden says you can keep the young swan here for a while if you can help him. But sooner or later the bird will have to go back to the Red Rock Lakes, where he belongs. The warden said he wouldn't let just *anybody* have a young swan, but he'd let *you* have one because you understand about birds, and he trusts you. That's quite a compliment, son.'

Mr Beaver looked pleased. Sam looked happy. Louis was greatly relieved. After a while everyone went in to supper in the kitchen of the ranch house. Mrs Beaver allowed Louis to stand beside Sam's chair. They fed him some corn and some oats, which tasted good. When Sam was ready for bed, he wanted Louis to sleep in his room with him, but Mrs Beaver said no. 'He'll mess up the room. He's no canary; he's enormous. Put the bird out in the barn. He can sleep in one of the empty stalls; the horses won't mind.'

A PUFFIN BOOK

stories that last a lifetime

Ever wanted a friend who could take you to magical realms, talk to animals or help you survive a shipwreck? Well, you'll find them all in the **A PUFFIN BOOK** collection.

A PUFFIN BOOK will stay with you **forever**. Maybe you'll read it again and again, or perhaps years from now you'll suddenly **remember** the moment it made you **laugh** or **cry** or simply see things **differently**. Adventurers **big** and **small**, rebels out to **change** their world, even a mouse with a **dream** and a spider who can spell – these are the characters who make **stories** that last a **lifetime**.

Whether you love animal tales, war stories or want to know what it was like growing up in a different time and place, the **A PUFFIN BOOK** collection has a story for you – you just need to decide where you want to go next . . .